STUMBLING INTO HIM

STUMBLING THROUGH LIFE BOOK ONE

MOLLY O'HARE

xoxo
Molly O'Hare

D1534200

Molly O'Hare

First Print: May 2018

Be You Publishing, LLC

www.MollyOHareauthor.com

ACKNOWLEDGMENTS

First, I want to thank YOU. Seriously, thank you!

Over the last few months I have met some amazingly supportive people in my life, and I couldn't do this without any of them. I am a better writer because of all of you. I want to thank my husband, for always having my back. My friend, my editor, and one of my biggest supporters, Karen. To my friends that supported me when I thought no one would. I love you, CBFFL. To my KB tribe: You have helped me so much. I don't know what I would do without any of you. I also want to thank Angela Verdenius. I am so honored to call her one of my good friends. I do not really know how to thank any of you other than offering to give you my undying love, which you already have. No take backs!

And, just for good measure. Thank you again... Okay, now I'll stop.

Fooled you... one more time: Thank you! – Come on, this is me we are talking about. Did you really think I'd stop?

DEDICATION

I dedicate this story to all of you. You are beautiful. You are strong. You are a unicorn. Do not let anyone tell you any different. The world is a better place because you are in it. This story goes out to anyone who never felt good enough or looked down upon for any reason. As I said in my last novel, rock who you are. There is only one you out there, so you might as well enjoy every second of it!
Stay awesome. Stay classy. And stay you!

CHAPTER ONE

"WATCH OUT!"

Holly Flanagan heard a commotion coming from the other side of the park.

Ignoring the shouting, she bent over focusing on picking up her Corgi, Waffles', most recent deposit. With Holly's track record, though, she should have known anyone yelling "watch out," "take cover," or "that's about to fall" was directed at her. Even after years of being the spokesperson for unlucky, klutzy, and clumsy she still disregarded the shouting as she carried on with her dog parent duties.

Before she could register what happened, she was knocked onto her back with a pain radiating from her mouth and nose.

"At least the sky is pretty today," Holly mumbled as she tried to get her bearings. She reached for her mouth as she felt the pain start to spread.

"Ma'am, are you okay?"

Holly closed her eyes as she thought about it.

Was she okay? She'd just been hit with something. She was pretty sure some part of her face, she didn't know which part, but she was sure something was bleeding. Waffles barked uncontrollably, and her head hurt.

So, was she okay?

Holly let out a heavy sigh.

Yeah, she was fine. This was just another day in her life for her. And so far, if being hit by an unknown projectile to the face was the worst thing that happened to her, she'd considered it a good day.

Deciding to face the music she opened her eyes.

Holy shit!

Above her, only a mere few inches from her face was by far the most handsome man she had ever laid eyes on.

He had dark brown hair and deep blue eyes that were richer than the ocean. His jaw was chiseled, with a light dusting of scruff, in the alpha male, I'm in charge here kind of way.

Wonderful. Okay, let's add embarrassing yourself in front of a Greek God to your list of attributes for the day. Hey, it can only get better from here, right?

When she realized she'd been staring at him for what could have been considered too long, she quickly jerked her head forward trying to right herself. Unfortunately for her, though, she slammed her head right into the Greek God's forehead.

Freaking wonderful.

Not only was her mouth hurting, her head now pounded.

Absolutely freaking wonderful!

"Shit," she heard the Greek God say as the wave of pain coursed through her body.

Taking the chance, she opened her eyes again only to see her Adonis holding his head. *Great.* And to make matters worse, Waffles started barking directly at her before looking at his recent deposit still on the ground then back at her.

"For the love of all things, dog. I was trying to pick it up," she growled, before taking her hand away from her mouth to deal with his majesty, *Lord* Waffles. However, the second her hand came into view she saw the blood and screamed.

"Oh shit. Lady, you're bleeding," the Adonis said, putting his hand under her chin moving it from side to side as he examined her face.

"What happened?" Panic ran through her. *Did I break my nose? Am I unconscious? Am I dying?*

The Adonis tilted her chin back to get a better look. "I was tossing the Frisbee with Ripley, and somehow it veered off course. I tried to warn you with the 'watch out.'"

Typical. Holly groaned. *Hot guy throws Frisbee. Said Frisbee hits me in the face. Hot guy then insinuates it's my fault for not getting out of the way fast enough. I mean, I know I'm generally invisible to men like him, but, damn. You'd think these extra wide hips would make me more visible.* She glared at the Frisbee sitting next to her.

Ignoring the object, she moved her eyes back to the Adonis.

"I can't tell if it's a busted lip or worse." He tilted her head further back like she was a child.

Holly ripped her face from his hand. She'd be able to tell if it was just a busted lip. She'd had too many to count in her life, from falling down, objects to the face, and even falling up the stairs. She reached into her pocket and pulled out the napkin she had stuffed in there from her soft pretzel. She blew off some stray salt and started feverishly wiping at her mouth.

"Let me see," he demanded, before taking one of the napkins from her hand. He then started dabbing at her lips.

She froze.

Well, Holly. This is the most action you've had in months. And, if some hot guy is all over you, you might as well enjoy it while it lasts.

Waffles crawled onto her lap demanding attention and started kissing the underside of her jaw.

Thanks, Waffles, for bringing the attention of my double chin to the Adonis. She rolled her eyes.

"Thanks for trying to help me clean up your mom," the Adonis remarked before quickly abandoning his job of cleaning the blood off her mouth to pat Waffles on the head.

"He's not trying to help you," Holly scoffed. "He's *trying* to remind me I still need to pick up his poop and then give him a treat."

"Shouldn't your mom be the one getting the treat if *she's* the one picking up your shit?" He cocked his head at her dog.

Waffles, ever the one to argue, looked at the man that now had a mischievous grin on his face, with the most judgmental side-eye he could muster.

No one came between him and his treats.

Ignoring Waffles' attempt at a threat, the Adonis once again pat the dog on the head before moving back to Holly's mouth dismissing him. "I think it's just a busted lip, but your front tooth..." He coughed as he sheepishly looked away.

"My front tooth?" Holly quickly ran her tongue along her front teeth. Shit, she felt a jagged piece. "Oh, crap." She quickly pulled her phone from her pocket and launched the front-facing camera.

As soon as she saw her face, she jerked back. Her hair

was all over the place, her face red, there was still blood on her...

You've had better days, Holly. She took a deep breath before he hastily opened her mouth to see the damage.

"Oh no."

Staring back at her was a chipped front tooth along with a busted lip. *Wonderful. Thank you so much, Universe. Thank you, so very much.* She didn't know whether she wanted to laugh or cry. *Clumsy Holly, strikes again. Do you ever take a break?*

As her eyes flooded with tears a sudden cold nose hit her arm distracting her. Realizing it wasn't Waffles she looked to her left and saw one of the most beautifully colored gray and black Australian Shepherds she'd ever seen.

"Aren't you a cutie?" she softly said. Thankfully, her love of animals overrode everything she was feeling.

"That's Ripley." The Greek God chuckled. "I'd thought you'd be more concerned about your mouth than a dog."

Ignoring him, she reached out to scratch Ripley's chin. "You're so pretty." Ripley must have agreed because she barked before kissing Holly's hand.

"Uhh, ma'am, I'm not a human doctor but I think we should pay more attention to your injuries instead of the dogs."

"Human doctor?" Her brows shot up. "As opposed to what, an alien doctor?"

"I haven't worked on any aliens that I know of, but I did neuter a cat named Alien once. Does that count?"

Her eyes widened at the realization. "Oh great, you've got a body of a Greek God, and now you're also a vet. Which of course means you love animals. *Freakin'* wonderful. You're like the most perfect guy, and here I am on the sidewalk with blood pouring out of me with a chipped tooth." She pushed Waffles off her lap and stood. "Please excuse me while I find a place to die of embarrassment."

A corner of the sexy man's mouth lifted. "You're funny."

"And you're hot. So, we've now successfully established which groups we belong to." Annoyed at herself more than anything she angrily started to stomp away from the Greek God.

"Hey, wait up!"

She spun around to glare at him. When Holly saw Waffles sitting at the foot of the Adonis looking up at him, her left eye started to twitch.

Of course, her dog would betray her. She wouldn't expect anything less. "Waffles, come." She pulled on the leash slightly, but the dog wouldn't move. "Lord Waffles, get your butt over here."

The man cocked his brow. "Lord Waffles?"

"Yeah," she answered. "He thinks he's a freakin' king. Hence the "lord" and I love waffles. Do you got a problem with that, buster?"

The Adonis burst into laughter as he scratched Waffles on the back. To make matters worse, that betraying Corgi rolled over onto his back asking for belly rubs.

The Audacity! *That's it. No more treats for you!* She glared at her dog.

"Who's a good boy?" the Adonis cooed. "You've got a weird name, but you're the best boy aren't cha?"

Holly's eye started to twitch harder.

She stomped back toward her bastard of a dog and the Greek God when out of nowhere her foot hit an invisible rock causing her to trip. Within a split second, she ended up falling right into the arms of the bane of her existence at the moment.

"Whoa, are you okay?"

"I'm fine," she grumbled as she righted herself. *Go ahead and add this to the, "it can only happen to me" list.*

"I feel like you need to walk around with a warning sign or at least a crash helmet," he joked.

"Not the first time I've heard that." Quickly she bent down and retrieved Waffles. "If you'll excuse me. Not only do I really need to find a secluded place to die of embarrassment, I also need to call my dentist, or go to the walk-in. Maybe both." She turned on her heel and started power walking down the sidewalk.

As she passed the spot she'd tripped at, she examined the cement. Figures, there'd be absolutely nothing there. If there were a sporting category on tripping over invisible objects she'd win gold twice over.

"Hey!"

She kept walking, doing her best to hide her humiliation and ignore the Greek God.

Unfortunately, that was short-lived. "Hey, I want to make sure you really are okay," he said, as he caught up to her in two point three seconds.

Stupid short legs! "I'm fine."

"Your lip's still bleeding."

She glared at him. "Wonderful."

"Hey..." He reached for her arm stopping her escape.

"What?"

"Let me help you. My practice is only a block from here. I've got all the supplies to clean up your lip. I can also get a better look at your tooth."

"You're a vet." Her eyes started to twitch again. *Could today get any worse?*

"I am pretty sure if I can surgically remove nuts from an animal I can look at your busted lip." He shrugged before smirking at her.

A laugh escaped her lips. He did have a point after-all. "Thank you for the offer...." she trailed off.

"Ben. The name's Ben Richman." He held out his hand to her.

"Thanks for the offer Dr. Richman, but there is a walk-in clinic not far from where I live."

"Call me Ben. And please let me do this. It'll help me sleep at night knowing the woman I maimed with a Frisbee is somewhat okay." She watched as his eyes pleaded with her. Even Waffles, the jerk, who was still in her arms looked up at her and whined. "Oh, for the love of... fine. Lead the way, Ben."

"Perfect." Ben's mouth curved into a smile. "Follow me."

When he whistled Ripley sat instantly by his side. He quickly bent down and fastened her leash before walking toward the street.

Holly looked at Waffles who was clearly enjoying being carried. "Guess you get an extra trip to the vet."

She couldn't help but burst out laughing when Waffles closed his mouth and glared at her.

CHAPTER TWO

For some strange reason Ben's heart hadn't stopped racing since the moment he saw the Frisbee head directly toward the lush woman bending over. Thankfully, his clinic was less than a five-minute walk from the park, but right now it somehow felt like an eternity.

He secretly glanced over his shoulder. The woman, whom he had yet to find out her name, held her Corgi in her arms all the while she seemed to be having a silent argument with the pup. He did his best to suppress his smirk. Those two were perfectly suited for each other.

As she was shooting death glares at Lord Waffles – *seriously, who names their dog Lord Waffles?* — he looked at her lip. Fortunately for them, the cut had stopped bleeding. She still had some dried blood on her chin, but that didn't distract from her beauty, though.

She was absolutely stunning. If he had to guess, he'd say she was around five-foot-seven, maybe a little shorter. She also had long dark brown hair that'd been naturally highlighted by the sun. Her eyes were a deep shade of hunter green, a color he'd never seen before.

He flicked his eyes appreciatively over her body. Her curves went on for days and that was exactly how he liked them.

Ripe and full.

The guy in him couldn't stop his imagination. Her breasts would overflow his palms nicely, and he was sure her ass would do the same. The moment he felt his lower half start to awaken, he scolded himself. *Nice going, Ben. Could you be any more of a creep?*

"Stop glaring at me, Waffles."

He looked at her face before looking at the pup. These two were quite the pair. He laughed.

Her quick wit and fun demeanor were no match for the over-opinionated Corgi.

A soft smile spread across his face. A sense of humor *and* beautiful.

Perfect.

"Yo, Dr. Ben, you got eyes on the side of your face? How do you even know where you're walkin' if you're staring at Waffles and me the whole time?"

Busted.

"Just making sure you're not still bleeding."

She quickly wiped the back of her hand against her mouth. "Am I?"

"Not that I can tell."

"Good. How much farther do we have to walk?" She looked at Waffles. "He takes after his mama. Not the lightest."

Ben stopped walking before turning toward her. His brows drew together.

"What?" she asked.

Did she just call herself fat?

Before he could question her, she tripped over a crack in the sidewalk.

"What the —"

Thank the Universe for his instincts. In less than a second, he caught Waffles who was flying through the sky and was able to use his body to keep the klutzy woman from falling onto her face once again.

"Lady, you've got to be the most uncoordinated person I've ever met."

As she righted herself, she pushed the hair out of her face. "Thanks for the insight, now I can die fulfilled knowing I am once again the winner of the clumsy award." She breathed heavy, making her chest rise and fall. Ben had to force himself to look into her eyes. *Holy shit, even when she's a mess, she's beautiful.*

"How much farther is your office?" she asked before plucking her dog out of his arms.

Feisty. He liked it.

Ben pointed to the sign across the street that read 'Richman Veterinarian Hospital.' He gave Waffles a quick pat on the head, before doing the same to Ripley. "Right over there, Grace."

"That's not my name!"

A smirk appeared on Ben's face. "No? Well, it should be since you're so *graceful.*" He held back his laugh as he saw her left eye start twitch.

"My name is *not* Grace." She pushed past him as Waffles sent him the side-eye. "It's Holly. Ya jerk."

Holly walked into the clinic and turned to see Ben staring at her from the front door. His eyes were gleeful, and his smile stretched from ear-to-ear. "Grace suits you better."

She glared at him.

"But, I like Holly, too."

"I'm glad you approve of my name. Now, can we please get this over with?" She tapped her foot.

Holly was still wreaking her brain at the idea there was a vet clinic here. How had she missed it? She'd driven and even walked up and down this street tons of times. Well, in her defense she was usually looking down making sure she wasn't going to trip, but she would have known if she'd seen a veterinarian's office. Ehh, she would definitely need to be more observant. Especially, if hot vets were roaming around in the city.

Ben smirked as he walked into the clinic. "Make yourself at home, Grace."

Instinctively, Holly kicked out her foot while he walked past her effectively tripping him. When he caught himself, he nodded at her, impressed. "Well played."

Holly raised her eyebrows triumphantly. "One point for Holly. Now, Doc Ben, I would like to get this over with."

"Oh, you sure are a fun one." He shook his head with a chuckle. "Do you think you can walk back to exam room one without breaking an arm?"

"Very funny." Holly ignored him as she made her way towards the room marked one. Unfortunately for her the weight of Waffles in her arms, combined with his panic of being at a vet's office unbalanced her. Before she could adjust her dog, she ended up falling into the door which swung open. "Oh for the love of—"

"I thought you said you could do it without breaking something?"

Holly righted herself before putting Waffles on the floor. "I didn't break anything!"

Ben's eyebrows arched as he walked into the room behind her. "Yet."

"I don't have to stand here and take this." Holly bent at her waist to retrieve the shaking Waffles. "Let's go, baby. We can head to the urgent care."

Before Holly even touched her dog a warm hand grasped her shoulder. "Hey, I'm just joking with you. You know, trying to lighten the mood in what could have been a terrible situation."

After a few seconds, she sighed. He was right. She was taking her anger out on him and he didn't deserve it. Even if he did call her Grace.

Her shoulders sunk in. No matter how many lucky pennies she carried or good luck charms she had Holly was always the one at the short end of the stick. Plus, she had so many other worries rolling around in her head. Now adding the busted lip and chipped tooth did not help anything.

Taking a deep breath, she did her best to center herself. All this man was trying to do, was help her.

Plus, she couldn't really blame him for poking fun at her. She was a walking disaster ninety-nine percent of the time. "You're right."

Ben stared at her like he was studying her. When he reached out for her chin, the intensity she saw in his eyes caused her to swallow.

"I'm always right, or at least I try to be," he spoke softly.

He gently stroked her lip with his thumb.

This had to be a dream or some weird reverse Hollywood movie. The kind where the hot guy falls for the unpopular and unattractive girl.

Ben removed his thumb from her lip and slowly traced it down her chin never once breaking their gaze.

Then she heard it.

The telltale sign of one, Lord Waffles, marking his territory. Holly snapped her face around. "Really, Waffles, really?" She glared at her dog trying to regroup. *I know the lust in his eyes was all in my head, but did you have to bring me back to reality so soon, Waffles?*

Ben barked out a laugh. "Gotta love dogs." He lowered himself to his knee, which caught Waffles' attention. Within less than a second, that betraying bastard was at Ben's side begging for belly rubs.

Holly's eyes narrowed on her dog. *No piece of bacon for you! Ever again.*

"It's okay, boy," Ben laughed while he scratched Waffles. "Us men need to mark our territory."

"Men do *not* need to mark their territory."

Ben looked back at her. "Sure, we do. It's how we get the word out."

Holly shook her head. "Hell no. No one's ever gonna pee on my leg to mark their territory," she said with utter disgust at even the thought of it. "And, if someone ever tried, I'd rip off his dick and make him eat it."

Ben let out one of the most genuine deep laughs she had ever heard.

"I like you, Grace."

When she lifted her arm as if to punch him, he held up his hands in surrender. "I mean Holly. You're funny. And, I wasn't saying men have to *pee* on items or people to mark what's theirs. That could be done lots of ways."

"Oh yeah?" she questioned crossing her arms over her chest. "And, what do you suppose that is?"

"Well, for starters, a wedding ring would do a pretty

good job, maybe a tattoo declaring their undying love for the other person."

Holly rolled her eyes. "I'd never be foolish enough to get a tattoo of someone's name on me." She wasn't going to admit the idea of having her husband tattoo *her* name on him sent shivers down her spine.

In reality though, she knew if she ever did get a tattoo with her luck the ink wouldn't take or worse... She'd most likely develop some infection and the entire body part she'd tattooed would end up having to be surgically removed. No, thank you. She was not taking that chance. She knew how the cards fell for her.

"Men aren't the only ones that can mark," he continued, ignoring her as the tension in the room shifted. "My favorite marks are scratches down my back."

Heat flooded Holly's cheeks.

Ben stood taking a step closer to her.

What in the world was going on? She fought the urge to look around for the cameras. She had to be on some prank show. "Yeah, well, I'd think a vet would be better equipped to detain his patients so he *wouldn't* be scratched."

As soon as the words were out of her mouth, her face paled. *Oh, God, Holly. Good going. Why are you so awkward! Now, he probably thinks you're into all the handcuffs and other stuff. Why do I have no brain to mouth filter?*

Ben's eyes darkened. "Maybe you're right."

"Nope!" Holly backtracked. "No, I'm not right at all. I am so far from being right; I'm left. Oh, look over there." She pointed behind him. When he turned, she bent and tried to pick Waffles up.

Ben laughed again. "You are something else, Holly." He nodded toward the exam table. "Come on, let's have a look at you."

Holly glanced at the table and then to Ben. Did he really think she'd get up there? The exam table was higher than her hips. She then looked at the one metal pipe holding the table in place. There was no way in hell that thing would hold her weight.

Ben must have read her mind. "It's weighted for four hundred and fifty pounds. I don't just get domestic animals in here. I've been known to perform surgeries on pot belly pigs."

"Did you just call me a pot belly pig?"

His eyebrow rose.

"Okay fine, even if it was weighted with some industrial enforcing secret ninja strength mechanism, how do you suppose I get up there?"

Before she knew it, Ben's hands were on her hips lifting her onto the table. "Well, okay then."

He smirked.

The confidence radiating off Ben sent shock waves through her. His jawline was intense but somehow inviting. She had the urge to reach out for it. As she felt her arm start to move a growling commotion on the floor snapped her out of whatever spell she was under. *What the hell is wrong with you, Holly Flanagan? Get it together. This insanely hot vet is not flirting with you!*

Shaking the thoughts from her head, she looked to the dogs who were now wrestling.

A chuckle from Ben diverted her attention once again. "Come on, Holly." Ben reached for the extendable light attached to the wall. "Let's take a look at the damage."

CHAPTER THREE

BEN PIVOTED the light so it was directly in front of Holly's mouth.

His heart still slammed against his chest. He didn't know what came over him, but the second she questioned getting onto the exam table he jumped at the chance to assist her. And he was sure as hell glad he did. Her hips molded to his hands perfectly. He had to stop himself from slipping his fingers under her shirt to feel her skin.

Get it together, Ben. Damn.

Okay, she was beautiful but this was unusual behavior for him. There was just something about Holly that ignited every nerve ending he had.

Right now, the only thing he wanted to do was explore all the possible reasons why. Maybe it was her quick wit, her adorable clumsiness, or her insanely delicious curves. Whatever it was, he wanted to drown himself in it.

Taking a deep breath, he commanded his body to control itself. "Close your eyes, Grace. I don't want the light to blind you."

Ben was instantly rewarded with her defiant glare. *Oh, she sure is fun to rile.*

"I will sic Waffles on you in a heartbeat." She gave him another dirty look.

"Do you mean the same Waffles that's licking my leg right now?"

Holly looked at the floor, her eyes narrowing before shooting back at him. "He's faking you out. He's trying to trick you into believing he is as sweet as maple syrup, but as soon as I give the command he'll attack."

"Is that so?"

To make a liar out of her, Waffles rolled onto his back and demanded a belly rub.

He laughed. This woman was something else, and as her death glared hardened even further on him he realized he hadn't had this much fun in months.

"Don't you have a job to do?" she demanded, snapping him from his thoughts.

Oh, he liked this. Ben laughed harder, placing his hand on his stomach. "Yes, your highness, I do. Now close your eyes and let me take a look."

When Holly *finally* listened to him and closed her eyes, he got a better look at her mouth. There was one cut a little under a half of an inch wide on her bottom lip. Carefully he used his fingers to move around the tissue looking for any other damage. He instinctively started caressing the side of her lip that didn't have the cut. And try as he might, he couldn't stop himself from imagining what it would feel like to have his lips pressed against hers.

Quickly, he averted his gaze to the wall. *What the absolute fuck is going on with me?* No one ever enticed these reactions from him before.

Taking a deep breath, he focused. As he examined her

upper lip he noticed a smaller laceration. Thankfully, neither cut seemed to need stitches.

Moving into work mode, he pulled out some cotton balls and cleaning solution from the drawer. He then took one of the saturated swabs and started wiping away the dried blood.

"Ouch, you jerk."

"This is the exact reason why I went the animal route instead of the human route," he said, ignoring her as he worked cleaning up the cuts.

"Why, because humans fight back?"

"If you think animals don't fight back you are sorely mistaken," he answered. "Animals don't run their mouth while I'm trying to fix them."

"I wasn't running my mouth. I explained what you were doing hurt."

His heart stopped. He'd hurt her? As he was about to apologize he saw the faint smile on her lips as her eyes danced with glee. That little shit was messing with him. "Sure thing, Grace," he said retaliating.

Instantly her face changed from smug to annoyance. "Jerk."

Ignoring her, he continued. "Open, Grace. Let me take a look at your tooth."

Holly crossed her arms over her chest, but did as he asked.

When she opened her mouth, he was able to see the chipped front tooth clearly. From what he could tell there weren't any cracks. He moved the tooth around to see if it was loose.

When he was done he turned off the light and pushed it back toward the wall. He then removed his gloves with a snap, causing both of the dogs to turn his way. "Well, Grace, your lips will survive to bring enjoyment to unexpecting patrons another day." Her eyes started to twitch again... Maybe he really should have her go to the urgent care in case something was wrong with her brain.

"That's good to know," she grumbled.

"Yup, no stitches. Your tooth on the other hand—"

She threw her hand to her mouth. "Am I gonna die?"

"You're pretty dramatic, anyone ever tell you that?"

"Am I gonna die is a legitimate question for someone that finds herself in certain positions more times than not."

Ben chuckled. "And, what might those positions be?"

When her eyes narrowed, he held up his hands in surrender. "Like I was saying, your tooth has a chip in it, but I don't see any cracks. Which is a good thing. I'm not a human dentist, but no cracks mean your tooth should be fine. I'm sure a dentist can easily add some composite to the chipped part, and you'll be good as new." Ben turned away from her retrieving his phone from his pocket.

"All you see is a chip?"

He didn't look up from his phone as he answered. "Yeah. I also moved your tooth around. There is some looseness, but nothing to be too concerned about. I don't think you'll have any lasting issues with it."

"Do you always ignore your patients?"

He finally looked from his phone he saw she was glaring at him with her arms crossed. "I'm not ignoring you. I'm setting up a dentist appointment for you."

"You're what?" Holly's eyebrows shot to the ceiling.

"That's the next logical step. I'm trying to see if he can get us in today."

Did he just say us? Holly's head spun as she tried to make sense of what was happening. "What do you mean *us?*"

Ben leaned against the counter across from her. He crossed his legs as he furiously typed on his screen. "We'd have to drop the dogs off at my house first, so not them."

"Whoa." Holly threw her hands up. "You need to take a step back. I am not dropping my dog off anywhere that isn't in my apartment. Besides, I am not going to some random crackpot dentist."

That dang smirk appeared on his face again as he looked at her. "I can't wait to tell John you said he was a crackpot. It'll make his day."

"I am not going to your dentist."

"Why not?"

"Because I don't know him. Hell, Ben, I don't even know you."

He put his phone down and opened his arms. "What do you want to know, I'm an open book."

"That's not what I meant." She took a calming breath. "I appreciate what you are trying to do, but I really just need to get out of here." She looked around the room for something to help her get down from the table.

Ben must have read her mind again because his hands were back on her hips before placing her safely on the ground. "John's my best friend. Let me help you here, Holly. I feel horrible that it was my miscalculation with the Frisbee that caused all of this. I want to fix it."

To make matters worse, her betraying dog plopped his big butt next to Ben's foot and whined at her agreeing with him. She narrowed her eyes at the loaf of bread. *Do you not understand,* I'm *the one who feeds you?*

When Waffles sent her a death glare that rivaled her own, her tongue had mindlessly touched her front tooth.

Dang it.

She ran her tongue over her tooth one more time. She knew the chip wasn't that bad, but she also knew she wouldn't be able to stop touching it with her tongue.

She closed her eyes. Could she deal with the possibility of cutting her tongue on the jagged edge? Opening her eyes, she saw a picture-perfect scene. Ben was on his knees with Waffles on his right, and Ripley on his left, all three of them had the puppy dog look on their faces. "Fine, you know what, let's go to your guy, but I swear if he turns out to be some weird dealer on the black market trying to harvest my appendix, tell him it was removed years ago. Oh, and I will murder you."

Ben plucked her dog into his arms who happily ate up the attention. "You mean you'll finally sic Lord Waffles on me?"

She was going to kill them both.

CHAPTER FOUR

BEN WATCHED Holly from the corner of his eye as they sat in the waiting room. She bounced her leg nervously as she pretended to be focused on an old magazine in her hands. There was something about Holly he couldn't quite put his finger on. He couldn't help but feel enamored by her.

Everything about Holly screamed adorable. Especially right now, every few seconds she'd shift her weight in the seat trying to relax. Maybe she wasn't a fan of going to the dentist? Or maybe —

Then she did it again.

Fuck me. Ben did his best to bite back his groan. Holly ran her tongue across her plump bottom lip, feeling the laceration. His heart raced as he couldn't stop himself from imagined it being *his* tongue. He'd gladly kiss away the pain. Or better yet, he'd kiss along her jawline being cautious of the tender spots. He'd make it his soul mission to distract her with his hands— *Jesus fucking Christ, Ben. Calm the fuck down.*

He was even starting to scare himself. He needed to get a grip. The poor woman had been through a lot today, and she didn't need him fantasizing about her to add to it. It didn't matter the raw lust he was feeling toward Holly was a new sensation to him. Sure, he'd lusted after beautiful women before, who hadn't? But with Holly, his nerve endings came alive and he had absolutely no idea why. But he sure as hell wanted to find out.

Ben continued to stay focused on her lips. He was soon rewarded for his ogling. Within less than a minute her little pink tongue snuck out of her mouth to touch her lip again.

Did she not understand what that did to him? Right now, his dick pressed so tightly against the front of his jeans, he was about to explode.

"Yo, earth to Ben, can you hear me?"

Jarred out of his thoughts, he looked at her. He felt his cheeks slightly heat. *Get it together, dude.* Clearing his throat, he sat straighter in his seat tugging on the front of his pants, desperately trying to make more room. "Uh, yeah."

Holly raised a brow.

No pulling the wool over her eyes apparently. "You caught me. I honestly have no idea what you were saying."

"Ben, this is serious."

The panic he saw in her eyes acted like a bucket of cold water being thrown on him. He uncrossed his legs moving his body a few inches closer to her. "What's the issue?" He knew no matter what was upsetting her, he'd do anything to fix it. It didn't matter the cost, if it were within his power to fix, he'd fix it. "What can I do?"

"For the love of all things, you weren't even a quarter listening."

"I already said I wasn't, Grace, now tell me what's got your panties in a bunch?" The glare she shot him went straight to his crotch.

Focus, dumbass.

"Do you think Waffles and Ripley will be okay at your house? I've never left him alone with another dog. What if he thinks Ripley is out to steal some scrap of food that was left on the floor and they fight to the death?" She worried her lip between her teeth. "Ouch."

Without questioning his gut reaction, he reached for her lip, pulling it from her mouth. "Careful, Holly. It's stopped bleeding for now, but you can easily break it open again." He used the opportunity to caress the sensitive tissue briefly before pulling away. "Ripley is a well-trained dog, but she's also a huge couch potato when she's at home. I can guarantee you right now she's sleeping on the couch, probably with her legs in the air."

"How can you be sure there isn't a food scuffle going on at this moment?"

His heart warmed. Someone this concerned about her dog was an animal lover, he had no doubts about it. Another point for Holly in the "pro" column. "Ripley is the best vacuum cleaner you will ever find. Every nook and cranny of my house has been well accounted for. I can assure you there will be no food scuffles."

"But aren't you not supposed to leave animals that just met by themselves?"

"Technically, as a DVM I would say yes. However, I was watching the way they interacted. There were zero signs of aggression. Not only that, Ripley is a certified therapy dog. If there is a high-stress situation, she defuses it pretty quickly. Or, if she feels the best course of action is to remove herself from the situation, then she will."

Holly's eyes still showed her concern. "You think they're okay?"

"I can prove it."

Ben pulled out his phone before opening his home security app.

When he looked at the screen he laughed. "See, Grace. Exactly like I told you." He handed her the phone. Ripley laid precisely where he said she would be. On her back with all four paws in the air, sleeping away. Waffles on the other hand, though, was trying with all of his might to jump onto the chair in the corner of the room. Unfortunately, for him his little Corgi legs didn't help.

"My poor baby," Holly cried.

Ben looked at the video feed again. Waffles backed up a few feet then ran with all of his might trying to jump onto the chair. Waffles: Zero. Chair: One, or however many times the poor guy had tried to jump onto the cushion. They watched as once more Waffles went through the motions, however this time, when he jumped his stomach hit the chair causing him to be flipped onto his back.

"Waffles!"

"He's fine." Ben chuckled at the Corgi. "Watch."

Waffles gave up his stance on sitting on the chair and moved to the dog bed by the wall.

"Crisis averted."

"For now," Holly grumbled.

"Let's do something to take your mind off everything," he suggested.

Holly turned all her attention on him. "Okay, like what?"

"Tell me about yourself?"

"There's not much to tell."

"Sure, there is." Ben once again crossed his legs. "Where do you work, what are your hobbies, have you ever been arrested, do you have a boyfriend?"

Holly scrutinized him for a second before throwing her head back in laughter. "You are something else, Benjamin."

His body froze. "Don't call me that. That's what my mother calls me."

She studied him. "Oh, that is definitely something we are going to explore."

"Not on your life."

"Oh, yes, Benjie. Friends talk to each other. Isn't that what you kept insinuating we are... Friends, that is?"

"Well, yeah." However, the last thing he wanted to talk about was his over botoxed, judgmental, bitch of a mother.

He needed to change the subject and fast. "I see you're avoiding the questions, is there something you're hiding, Holly?"

"Nothing to avoid. I work for the public library on Eighth and Johnson, I've been employed there for three years now, and I love it. No boyfriend, unless you count Lord Waffles. I love to read, hence working at the library. It's a dream job for me. I also like to write short stories here and there. I want to try my hands at writing a full novel. I really spend most of my free time taking care of my dad. As for being arrested, I plead the fifth."

So many questions and images were running through Ben's head. *A fucking librarian?* There was no way for her to be more perfect. His heart raced as fantasies of her being the dirty librarian ran through his head. He'd love to see her hair pulled into a tight bun, maybe some dark-rimmed glasses on her face. Her wearing a black tight pencil skirt with a white blouse. This time he didn't hold back his groan.

"You okay?"

Through his haze of lust, her other words dawned on him. "Wait, were you arrested?"

Her face flooded with heat. "Yes and no."

He uncrossed his legs before bringing his elbows to his knees leaning closer. "Explain."

"There isn't really a lot to explain. It was all a misunderstanding. Like today, I was in the wrong place at the wrong time."

"Keep going."

"It's nothing really. One day I decided I wanted to walk a new route home after work. You know, mix things up a bit. Well, I got a little lost and ended up in some back alley. After a few minutes of walking, I saw some guy leaning against a brick wall."

"Holly, please tell me you didn't."

"I thought they could help me get back on the right path. Before I knew it, I was being thrown against the wall and being told I was under arrest for buying drugs."

Ben shifted back into his chair and burst out laughing.

"It wasn't my fault and as soon as everything calmed down, I was released."

"You really are something else." Ben smiled from ear-to-ear. "Okay, so a felon you ain't. You said you take care of your dad during your free time, does he live close?"

Holly's face lit. Clearly, the mention of her dad made her happy. He couldn't help the slight chuckle that escaped him when she smiled showing her teeth. The chipped tooth and all.

"Yes, he only lives a few miles from me. I've been trying to get him to move in with me, though. But he swears he's still able bodied enough to live on his own. I don't agree, but it's like beating a dead horse. Eventually, he'll get the picture."

"Why do you want him to move in with you? If he's able to live on his own, I don't see a problem with it."

Once again, she worried her lip. "No, I understand what you're saying and he's still, for the most part, independent. It's just after he got hurt and couldn't go back to work, things took a turn for the worse. See, it's just him and me. We're all we've got in this world after my mom died when I was five."

Ben blindly reached for her hand, giving it a light squeeze. "I'm sorry to hear that."

"Don't be. We do just fine on our own. Most of my free time I spend helping him do things around the house that he can't do anymore. I always make sure his pantries are stocked, and he has everything he needs until I can get back over to him."

"You sound like a good daughter."

"He's my dad. I'd do anything for him." Pain slashed through Ben's heart. He knew the feeling.

"Now that you know my sad life story, why don't you tell me all about you and why you apparently hate the name Benjamin?" Holly adjusted herself on her seat once again, smiling showing off her chipped tooth. *That little shit!*

As Ben opened his mouth to speak, one of the dental technicians came into the waiting room. "Holly Flanagan."

"Oh, boo." He jutted out his bottom lip. "I guess story time is over."

She gave him a dirty look. "I'll be back."

"I'm looking forward to it."

Over an hour later Holly's tooth was good as new. Well, for the most part. The dentist, or John as he liked to be called, was able to fix the chipped part with a composite. Although, he did warn her she needed to be careful with her tooth from now on. The fact there now was some damage apparently might weaken the tooth and could cause a crack. If that were the case, she might need to get her whole tooth fixed. Thankfully, that wasn't anywhere on the horizon for her.

Holly walked into the reception area and watched Ben stand and make his way toward her. "How'd it go?" he asked.

"Not as bad as I thought it was going to be. Like you said, he didn't see any cracks, and he was able to fix it."

"That's great." Ben's face brightened. "Did he say anything else? John's been known to never shut up. He has his hands in your mouth and he'd asked you questions like you could actually answer him."

A laugh escaped her. That was exactly what John had done. He'd be asking questions about everything and anything, and when she would try and answer, he'd tell her to keep her mouth open while he worked. "Not really, he only said I need to be careful about how I bite."

"Makes sense."

Holly leaned over the receptionist counter. "How much do I owe you?"

The lady behind the desk started typing on her computer. "Let's see." After thirty seconds she looked at Holly. "The total will be $698.98."

Holly blanched. *What the hell?* How could fixing a small chipped tooth cost that much? "Umm, can I ask why it's so expensive? I gave you my dental card when I came in."

The lady looked back at her screen. "Everything done today was considered cosmetic work and your insurance doesn't cover that."

"Oh." Holly heart sank. How was she going to pay for

this? As of right now, if she paid this bill she'd have all of five dollars left to her name. How could that last a full two weeks until she got paid again? And, what about her Dad? Every spare dime she had she put toward his medical bills. *Great, why does this crap always happen to me? Why can't I catch a break?*

Holly quickly tried to do some calculations. She went shopping two days ago. If she split all of her meals into three servings, she should be able to make it. Then she remembered her Dad's recent late notices. She'd been trying to work out a payment plan with the medical billing department but they weren't willing to help.

She was toying with the idea of getting an additional part-time job to help pay his bills. Maybe this was the gentle push she needed.

Shoving all those thoughts away, she took a deep breath. She had no other choice here. The work had already been completed on her tooth. She reached into her purse.

"Put it on here." Ben's voice shocked her.

"What are you doing?"

"What does it look like I'm doing?" He was giving his card to the lady. "I'm paying your bill."

"What do you mean you're paying my bill?"

"Exactly that. It was my mistake not watching where the Frisbee was headed. I should be the one to pay for this." Ben tried to hand the receptionist his card again.

"I don't care about that. I can pay my own way."

"I never said you couldn't."

"I'm not letting you pay for this, Ben. Plus, it's far too expensive." Which was true.

"I'm not taking no for an answer."

"What's all this commotion out here?" John, the lovely and sadistic dentist she'd just had the pleasure of meeting asked walking into the room. "Ben, what the hell is going on? You causing trouble?"

"We're having a lover's quarrel on who's gonna pay."

A lover's quarrel? I'll kill him.

John's eyes widened for a brief second, before pure glee clouded his face. "I see, buddy. Ms. Flanagan—"

"Holly," she corrected just as she had every other time he tried calling her Ms. Flanagan.

"Fine, Holly. Trust me when I say this, let Ben fit the bill."

"Exactly," Ben agreed.

"No."

"He can afford it." John winked at Ben.

"Yeah, well so can I," Holly countered. *Well sorta.*

"No, he really can afford it. Plus, he needs to put his money to good use, like my practice." John winked at Ben.

"You know, you could just comp the dental work," Ben remarked.

"And lose out on watching this, what did you call it, a lover's quarrel?"

"No one is comping anything." Holly turned toward the receptionist and handed over her card. "Here."

Ben yanked the card away. "Nope." He shifted his body so he was now completely facing Holly. "I'm paying for this. End of story." He held his hands up. "How about you buy me dinner to make up for it?"

Holly clenched her fists at her sides. This was getting her nowhere. You know what, if he wanted to pay, then fine. When she took him to dinner it would be the most expensive restaurant she could find... well, within her budget of course. "Fine. But, we're getting steaks."

"You know the exact words to make my heart flutter," he said before placing his hand on his head to fake swoon.

Yup, she thought. *I'm gonna find a way to make that steak have poison on it.*

"Told you, Holly, the Richman's *always* get their way," John said.

"And we always will."

"Remind me to tell that to your mother the next time she comes in and starts bitching about how you refuse to give up the silly animal job and work for the family business. She sucks all the good out of everything," John stated matter of fact.

Ben paled.

Before she could ask what was going on, recognition dawned on Holly. *Richman? As in Richman Industries?* She felt her stomach bottom out. *Holy Fuck.*

Holly's eyes widened. "You're a Richman."

CHAPTER FIVE

Holly walked as fast as she could along the city street. Right now, her primary goal entailed getting as far away from a *Richman* as possible. Doing her best not to trip on any invisible cracks she quickened her pace.

Universe, why do you hate me?

Tears welled in her eyes. Of all the people she could've made a fool out of herself in front of, it had to be one of the most influential people in the whole state.

Freakin' Richman Industries.

She blanched.

Good going, Holly.

"Grace, why are you running away?"

Because, I'm an idiot.

Ben instantly by her side. "Seriously, what's got you running like your ass is on fire? You do know John wouldn't have charged you right? He only did it 'cause he's my best friend and was messing with me." He laughed. "Plus, I don't think running down the street's a wise move for someone who's so..." He paused for a moment. "Shall I say accident-prone?"

Holly came to an abrupt halt and scowled at him. "It's not nice to make fun of people."

"I'm not making fun of you, Holly, I'm merely stating a fact." He placed one of his hands in the pocket of his jeans. "Now, explain to me why you took off out of the office like a bat out of hell?"

"I did not," she protested, crossing her arms over her chest.

Ben cocked his brow.

"Fine. I felt foolish, okay?" Her eyes fell to the ground as her face flushed.

"Why?"

Holly glanced at him. "Uh, I don't know. Maybe it has something to do with making myself look like a, how did you put it? Oh yeah, an accident-prone loser in front of someone who could be the most powerful man in the whole state?" She huffed. *Great, now you've just word vomited all over the man.*

Ben's face contorted. "I never once called you a loser."

"Semantics."

Ben quirked his head to the side. "No. It's not. I never and would never call you a loser, Holly. Sure, I might joke around with you, but I'd never say anything like that. I don't think you're a loser at all. Actually, I like all your qualities." His eyes darkened. "*A lot.*"

She couldn't help but roll her eyes. "Sure."

"Okaaaaay." Ben grabbed her arms and started moving her from side to side, looking all around her.

"What are you doing, you weirdo?"

"I'm trying to find the same girl I met at the park a few hours ago. Did she get abducted by aliens and you've been sent down to replace her?"

Holly jumped out of his grasp and scrutinized him. "You're strange."

Ben's eyebrows shot to the sky. "Says the one that might have been abducted."

Within that instant all of the tension she was feeling subsided. "You're something else."

"You ain't seen nothing yet." He threw his arm around her shoulder, pulling her into his side. "Now, how about we head to the store, pick up some food and we can cook dinner at my place."

"I don't think—"

"If I recall correctly," he said interrupting her. "You promised me a meal."

She stopped walking and turned toward him. "No, I agreed to take you out."

Ben's face brightened. "Oh, Grace. Did you just ask me on a date?"

She paled. "Wait, what? I never said that."

"No take backs. I accept." Ben pulled her to his side again, coaxing her to walk.

"I don't like being manipulated," she grumbled. Even though every fiber of her being wanted to throw his arm off and run in the opposite direction there was something about Ben that pulled her in.

"I'm not manipulating you, Grace. I'm simply agreeing to your terms," he stated as a matter of fact.

"Anyone ever call you a jerk?"

His eyes brightened. "All the time."

Holly's head still whirled as she sat at the island countertop in Ben's kitchen across from where he was preparing their meal. How did she get herself into these situations? Shaking her head, she looked at the red mark forming on her upper arm. The trip to the grocery store had been by far one of the most eventful experiences of her life. Which was saying something because every day was an experience for her. Maybe it was due to the fact Ben unnerved her or maybe she was still rattled by the events of the day? It seemed as though when she was around Ben, she ended up being even more of a klutz than she usually was.

In aisle eight, when she tried to reach the top shelf to get some of the fried onions, the whole shelf collapsed with all its products cascading onto her. She wasn't hurt other than a few red marks and after Ben got most of his laughs out, he righted her in one swift movement.

Then, when Holly tried to pay for their items, Ben growled at her. Honest to God growled at her. She'd never heard of that happening in real life. Sure, in her romance books she'd read it tons of times. But that wasn't real world stuff, at least that's what she thought.

Holly was only mildly annoyed he refused to let her pay. Even with her argument that she was the one supposed to be treating him to a meal, she bit her tongue and gave in. At that point, he still had her dog.

"Steaks will be done in few minutes," Ben announced, turning away from the food to face her.

Waffles and Ripley both barked in unison with their excitement causing Holly to roll her eyes. They both sat like picture perfect dogs at the edge of the island counter where she sat.

"Who said I'd share?" Holly directed her attention to Waffles who goofily stared back at her, his tongue dangling out of his mouth. He must have thought her words were an invitation because he trotted over to her legs and started licking her jeans. "You're such a weirdo, Waffles." She reached for his fluff burying her hands in his fur giving him a good scratch. "You know mommy will always give you anything you want."

"And that might be why he takes advantage of you," Ben chimed in as he moved the steaks to a plate he'd already prepared.

Holly glared. "Are you going to ignore that your dog barked, too?"

Ben pat Ripley on top of her head. "She knows she'll only get what I give her and not all the time. What kind of vet would I be if I fed her human food?"

Holly sheepishly looked at Waffles, then back to Ben. "Whoops."

Ben chuckled as he got the baked potatoes out of the oven.

As he finished preparing their meals Holly glanced around his kitchen. It was modest. Not at all what she would've pictured a Richman having. Mind you, it was bigger than her apartment, but it wasn't quite what she envisioned for the powerhouse name. Before she could stop herself, the words were out of her mouth. "If you're a Richman and deemed one of the richest families in the state why don't you live in a mansion or something by a lake?" She winced.

After placing the baked potatoes onto their plates, Ben turned toward Holly. "First, I'll never live on a lake. Mosquitoes are a bitch. Second, I'm not rich. My parents' company is rich, my *family* is rich, but I'm not. I live off of the income I make with my practice." He walked toward the island leaning both of his arms on the counter directly across from her. "Is this why you've done a one-eighty after learning I'm a Richman? You think having money is some sort of superpower?"

"Not at all, it's just that—"

"Holly, I want absolutely nothing to do with Richman Industries and as far as I'm concerned the place can burn to the ground."

Holly's eyes widened. "Wow."

"Yeah."

"Okay," she murmured. "I'm sorry I brought it up."

She watched as Ben's body stiffened. "Don't be."

"You don't get along with your parents, then?" she asked before hitting her head with her palm of her hand. "Don't answer that. Along with my clumsiness I seem to win the award of saying the wrong thing at the wrong time."

Ben chuckled. "And yet, I find that extremely adorable."

"Adorable." She rolled her eyes. "Yeah, right."

Ben's eyes darkened before leaning across the counter. His face was only inches from hers. "Oh, Holly, if you only knew what I thought about you."

She swallowed hard. *Abort, abort.* She had to do something. "Waffles has to pee!"

A half-smile appeared on his face. "That so?" He glanced at Waffles who was sitting at his feet looking toward him with pure devotion in his eyes. *I feel ya, Waffles. I'm enamored with the guy as well.*

"Do you have to go outside, boy?" Ben asked.

Waffles flopped over onto his back, giving Ben his belly. *Stupid dog.*

"I think he wants human food."

"Whatever," Holly grumbled. "What's the deal with your family? Do you really hate them?"

Ben scoffed. "It's not that I hate them, it's more of we

don't see eye to eye on a lot of things and I don't agree with ninety-eight percent of the shit my mother does."

"What about your father?" Holly questioned before reaching for her drink.

"My dad was amazing. He's the reason I'm here today."

Holly sat straighter on her chair. "You said was. Is he no longer around?"

Ben looked away before speaking. "No, Richman Industries killed him and I blame my mother for that."

Okay, Holly wasn't sure what can of worms she'd opened, but she was desperately looking for some sort of reverse can opener to put it back.

Ben must've seen the panic in her eyes, as he further stated, "He worked himself to the bone to please my mother, but she was never satisfied. Every dollar he earned, she wanted him to earn two more. Every present he bought her, she'd scoff at and demand something else. He worked his ass off and all that got him was a heart attack that led him to an early grave."

"Oh, Ben, I'm so sorry." Holly wasn't sure what else to say. She'd only known Ben a few hours, but for him to speak so personally with her, melted her heart. She fought the urge to run to him and pull him into her arms.

"Don't be sorry it wasn't your fault, it was my mothers."

The pain in his voice crushed her. "Now, I understand why you don't like her."

"Not liking her is an understatement. We don't see eye to eye on anything, and after my dad died, she demanded I take his place as CEO of the company."

"That's not what you wanted, right?" Holly asked.

"Hell no." Ben jerked back. "Whenever there's a reason I have to step into Richman Industries I get the heebie-jeebies." He shuddered. "I fucking hate that place. That's not the life I want. Since I was a kid, I've always been interested in animals. Everything about them fascinated me. From their loyalty to their unique personalities. They gave me unconditional love when no one else was able to. Even my dad was too busy pleasing my mother to be there for me. Animals were always there, though."

Holly's heart went out to Ben as she thought back to her own life. "I completely get it. After my mom died my dad got us a cat. I loved that cat more than anything in the world. I named her Princess Huffle Stuffle and she let me tell her all of my secrets. I loved her more than I ever realized. I was heartbroken when she was diagnosed with renal failure and passed away."

"You and the strange names you pick for your animals." Ben chuckled. He shook his head, before sighing. "Animals bring out a side of us that we didn't know we had. Animals can calm you. They can protect you and be a companion when you think the world is against you. My dad understood that. He never once pushed me to follow in his footsteps. On the contrary, he did everything in his power to help me achieve my dreams of owning my own veterinarian practice," Ben reminisced. "I remember the day I graduated from Veterinary Medicine and he handed me the deed to the building my practice is set up in. He told me he was proud of me and he wished he'd followed his own dreams." He shook his head. "Apparently, that caused a fight between my parents. She didn't understand why my dad wanted me to pursue happiness instead of joining the family business and making as much money as I possibly could."

Ben quickly turned away opening a drawer to retrieve their silverware. "I was never sure of her motives but I knew her pushing for me to be the head of the company is to solely benefit her." After closing the drawer, he handed Holly her plate. "My father wasn't even cold yet when my mother started knocking on my door demanding for me to take his place and make her more money."

"Shit." Holly bit her bottom lip, before remembering the cut. "Ouch. I, uh, don't even know what to say."

"You don't have to say anything. Honestly, I have no idea why I even told you all of this. I never talk about it. Plus, I've lucked out in life. I walk into my practice every day and know I'm following the path that was laid out for me."

Ben had a point. He clearly knew what he wanted out of life, and he wasn't afraid to pursue it. Holly wished she could say the same about herself.

"Now that I know more about you," Holly said, trying to lighten the mood. "I don't feel as creeped out that I'm sitting in your kitchen after only meeting you six hours ago. Eating a steak that might have been poisoned while my dog has decided you're a better human being than I am." She shrugged giving him a side smile.

Ben threw his head back and laughed after taking a bite of his food. "You make me laugh, Holly. I like that about you."

She smiled. "Maybe I should change my day job to be a clown?"

"Nah," he replied. "You're more the sexy librarian type." His eyes sparkled with mischief. "Speaking of that, what about that date you promised me?"

CHAPTER SIX

HOLLY SAT at her desk chewing on a pen cap. Every time she tried to focus on cataloging books, her mind would wander to Ben and their evening together. The events of yesterday still boggled her mind. How had she gone from walking Waffles in the park, to having dinner at the Adonis' house?

She shuddered.

Could she still call Ben her Adonis now that she knew him? A part of her thought it was weird, but then there was another part of her that liked it.

It was rare for someone like Ben to pay attention to someone like her. Okay so he was the reason for her having a chipped tooth and he probably felt guilty. His pity was more than likely the reason for his actions yesterday... Except there was something about Ben that made her want to believe his motives were honest.

Holly idly ran her tongue along her front tooth. Carefully, trying not to irritate her cut, Holly nibbled on her bottom lip, something she did while she was thinking.

When she closed her eyes, she could still feel the gentle

touch of Ben's fingertips as he examined her. She couldn't stop herself as she stroked her tongue over the cut. Leave it to her to be hit with a Frisbee, chip a tooth, and then be cared for by one of the hottest men she'd ever seen. Then that same man turned out to be a Richman.

Holly inadvertently cocked her head to the side as she thought. After talking with Ben she couldn't see him as a Richman anymore. Not with the way he loathed Richman Industries.

As Holly sat there at her desk her heart broke for him. It had to be rough living pretty much isolated from your family. She didn't know what it was like to be secluded from her loved ones. Her dad meant the world to her. Then again, Holly's dad was loving and supportive.

After hearing about Ben's mother, she couldn't blame him for distancing himself from her and Richman Industries. Once Ben finished telling her about his mother, all Holly wanted to do was find his mother and punch her in the nose.

Deciding it was best to leave it alone she thought back to Ben. How in the world was a man built to be that good looking?

Over conversation last night, he'd leaned forward on the table showcasing his solid arms. She almost died right then and there. Then there was the way he looked at her. It was unheard of in her book. The intense look in his eyes when he watched her made her heart race.

There was something about him that she couldn't ignore. Lord knows she was trying to. No man like him would ever be interested in a klutzy woman like her. And she knew that.

Sighing, she opened her eyes to get back to work. Might as well forget him. It was better that way.

"You better spill."

Holly jumped at the sound of Mildred her sixty-seven-year-old co-librarian. "What? You almost gave me a heart attack."

"You heard me, missy. There are only two things that can put that type of look on a woman's face. That's a man that knows what he's doing or food. And I don't see any food around you. So, you better start spilling your guts." Mildred pulled the rolling chair from her desk over to where Holly sat. "I've been waiting for the day I can start reliving my life through you. Normally, you've got your head so far up a book, I thought you were a crazy cat lady with a dried, shriveled up hoo-ha. But now, no sirree, Bub. That face right there is a face of a woman who knows she's got a man that can bring her to her knees and vice versa." Mildred waggled her eyebrows.

"Eww. God, Mildred. Do you have to be so crude?" Holly asked before turning away from the nosy woman back to her computer.

"Crude? I wasn't crude. It'd be crude if I asked how long his dong was."

"Mildred!"

"What?" She sat back in her chair crossing her legs. "Can I not ask how your day was yesterday?"

Holly pushed back from her desk turning toward her. "Of course, you can ask how my day was. I did the same thing I do every time I have a half day here. I go home and walk Waffles. That's about it."

Mildred cocked her head to the side. "That it?"

"Yes, that's it." Holly glared at her as laughter gleamed in her eyes. That was one thing she loved about the crazy old coot. She'd be the first one to call you on your bullshit. And, she'd also be the first one to back you up in a fight. She had more fire in her than Holly had seen in anyone.

"Is Waffles the one that's got your cheeks red, and your eyes filled with lust?"

"Mildred, my eyes are not filled with lust!" To her horror, she heard someone clear their throat from behind her. She instantly felt her cheeks heat. *Damn it, Mildred. This better not be old man Robins.*

Doing her best to ignore her embarrassment, Holly turned ready to apologize for shouting and ask the person what she could do for them. As soon as she saw who was standing there, she panicked. "Ben!"

"Is this the young man that's got your panties wet?"

Holly shot her head back to Mildred. "Enough, old woman! Back to your witch's cavern before I sic overdue calls on you." Holly did her best to be firm as her insides were a jumbled mess. Of all the things for Ben to hear, the nonsense out of Mildred's mouth about the state of her panties was not one of them.

Mildred's face lit. "Yup, this must be the man." She held out her hand past Holly. "Name's Mildred. Nice to meet you. I'm glad someone's finally dusted off the ol' cobwebs between Holly's thighs."

Ben roared with laughter as he shook Mildred's hand. "What can I say? I'm very satisfying." He winked.

Mildred turned toward Holly. "You should be lucky I'm not thirty years younger or I'd be jumping on him so fast it'd make both our heads spin."

"You're married," Holly reminded her.

"And?" Mildred winked before departing into the far end of the library.

"Please excuse Mildred, her old age has made her

senile. I think we're going to have to look into putting her into a home soon." Holly nervously laughed.

"Huh?" Ben smirked. "That's a shame. I liked her."

"Who doesn't?" Holly sat farther back in her chair before pushing the hair out of her face. "What can I do for you, Ben? What brings you to my neck of the woods?"

Ben's face brightened as he leaned his left hip onto her desk. "I was in the area and I figured I'd stop by and say hi."

She looked at him curiously.

"And, Ripley told me she missed Lord Waffles and wanted a playdate. What do you say to dinner and a movie tonight? Your choice."

"My choice in food or the movie?"

He scrunched his face. "You only get one choice: food or movie. I pick the other."

"How very chivalrous of you."

"I thought so."

"Why are you really here?"

"For the exact reason I just said."

"Your dog wants a playdate?"

"Yeah?"

Holly burst out laughing. "Sure, your pup wants a play-date. You can't even convince yourself."

Ben's face broke out into a ridiculously wide grin. "Well, when you put it that way I want a playdate too."

Holly raised her brow. "Do you want me to get Mildred?"

"Nah, she's undoubtedly too much woman for me."

"You're probably right."

"All joking aside, Grace..." She glared at him. "I had a good time yesterday, apart from hitting you in the face."

"You hit her in the face?" Mildred hollered from behind a bookshelf.

"Get back to work, you old lady!" Holly yelled back.

"You two are no fun."

"If I knew the library was this entertaining I would have spent more time in one rather than on the field." Ben shook his head.

"Of course, because you just had to be a jock, weren't you?"

"You say it like it's a bad thing." At her dirty look, he held his hands in surrender which caused her to narrow her eyes.

Ignoring her, he continued, "Anyway, I had a great time with you yesterday. I can't remember the last time I laughed as much as I did. I figured we could hang out again tonight if you're not doing anything."

"She's not doing anything!"

Holly shot her head to where she heard Mildred's voice. Low and behold the old coot was peering at them from in between a few books.

"As much as I would like to disagree with Mildred..." Holly turned back toward Ben. "I'm not doing anything. I only planned on working on a short story I'm writing and watching some reruns."

"Perfect." Ben stood bringing his hands together in a clap. "What time do you want to meet?"

Holly leaned over her desk looking at her schedule. "I promised I'd help update our electronic reader catalog tonight. I don't think I'll get out of here until around six thirty. I can run home and get Waffles and meet you at your house at seven fifteen."

"I get off at five today unless there's an emergency. How about I pick up something to eat, grab a movie, and meet you at your house when you get off? That way you won't have to worry about anything else other than going home."

Holly thought about it for a few moments. Did she want Ben to know where she lived? His boyish glee melted her heart. Plus, she hated feeling hurried. Whenever she felt rushed her clumsiness skyrocketed by one thousand percent. It'd be better for Ben to deal with everything, and Holly just show up. "You know what, that sounds pretty good." She took out a piece of paper and wrote down her address. "Here you go. Meet me outside of my apartment building at six forty-five."

"Deal." He reached around Holly grabbing her cell phone that was on her desk. He started fiddling with it before he gave the phone back to her. "My number's in there in case you need to call. I also texted myself, so I have yours as well."

She took her phone putting it in her pocket. "Okay, Ben. I'll see you later."

"Yeah," he said turning away. "I'll see you tonight." He looked over his shoulder and winked. "Maybe then we can talk about how I make your panties wet."

CHAPTER SEVEN

BEN SAT OUTSIDE of Holly's apartment building with Ripley by his side. He hadn't known what came over him throughout the day. When it hit lunchtime at the clinic before he knew it, he found himself headed toward the library. No plan in mind, all he knew was he wanted to see Holly.

He was pleasantly surprised when he walked in on the conversation Holly and her coworker were having. He thought he'd hit the jackpot.

Mildred was a hoot. Her foul mouth and crude remarks only made him like her more. It was to his advantage they were talking about him. Plus, how could he go wrong when wet panties were involved?

The mortification on Holly's face amused him beyond measure. You'd have thought she'd been caught with her pants around her ankles with her ass up in the air.

Instantly his lower half stirred to life as he bit back a groan.

Ripley sensing the change in her owner, leaned against his leg placing her head on his lap. Her ice blue eyes looked to him for guidance. "Sorry, girl. Your dad has somehow went and lost his mind."

Ripley whined.

"You're still my number one girl, Rip. Promise." Ripley's response was a tongue flop onto his right knee. Ben scratched her head ruffling her fur. "What would I do without you?"

"You'd probably be sitting out here talking to yourself." Ben looked from Ripley to see Holly making her way down the sidewalk.

Damn, she was beautiful. She wore a fitted long sleeve hunter green top with black pants that hugged her hips. Her hair was pulled on top of her head in a neatly placed bun. From what he could tell, she barely wore any makeup, if any at all. Holly was such a natural beauty and the fact she didn't see herself that way made his desire for her stronger.

Everything about her screamed lust, from her ample hips that begged for his hands to caress, to her incredible chest. Then there was the way she sashayed her hips from side to side as she walked. If he didn't know better, he'd have sworn she was trying to seduce him.

"Were you waiting here long?" she asked, reaching the steps to the lobby door.

"No," he choked out, before clearing his throat. *Get yourself together.*

"Hi, Ripley." Holly bent at her waist to greet his dog giving him a perfect view of her delectable ass. He had to control himself from reaching out and squeezing it. Closing his eyes, he fought the images of her bent over as he took her from behind. He let out a tiny groan.

"You okay?"

His eyes shot open. "Yeah." He shook his head. "Yeah, no, I'm fine."

"You looked a little weird there for a second."

He held up the take-out bag. "It's the food. I brought Chinese and the smell is making my mouth water. I'm starving."

"I didn't know food did it for you," Holly joked.

"Oh, Grace, many things do it for me." He held open the lobby door for Holly to walk in, once again giving him a perfect view of her ass. He held onto Ripley's leash and the food as they made their way to the elevator.

Once they were inside, Ripley couldn't contain her excitement. She trotted to be right next to Holly. When Holly turned to face him, she hadn't seen the leash which caused her to stumble into Ben's arms. Thankfully, he had quick reflexes.

"And you say Grace isn't the name for you?" he joked while righting Holly.

She brushed her shirt down before looking at him. "It's not." Holly lifted her chin and made her way inside the elevator. Damn, she's adorable when she's stubborn. It only made him like her even more.

"I live on the third floor." She pressed the button. When the doors closed, she descended to her knees to scratch Ripley. There she went again being perfect.

When the elevator door opened, they made their way to her apartment. When she opened the door, Waffles came running toward her. He started wagging his butt as fast as he could, while bark-whining his excitement that his mom was home.

"There's my big boy! Who's mommy's big boy?" she said as she eagerly welcomed Waffles into her arms.

Within seconds of their greeting, Waffles looked around Holly and stared at Ben and Ripley, whom at his command was sitting patiently at his side. Waffles took off in a full speed pursuit toward him and Ripley. Once his little legs made it to Ben, he jumped on him demanding pets.

Holly faced the commotion. "What am I chopped liver now?"

Ben laughed as he greeted Waffles. "What can I say, Waffles is a man's man."

"Whatever," Holly huffed before throwing her bag onto the nearby table. When Waffles turned his attention from him to Ripley, Ben took the time to examine Holly's home.

It was a relatively small apartment. The front door led right into the living room. The walls were a light shade of blue, with inspirational quotes that were framed and scattered all around. There was a decent sized couch in the middle of the room that had seen better days, with a second-hand coffee table in front of it. Everything appeared pretty tame. Which surprised him, Holly seemed anything but tame. Looking toward his right, he noticed a tiny kitchen that only had room for the essentials. Once again there were inspirational quotes on the walls accompanied by odd knickknacks.

Continuing his scan, he made his way into the middle of the living room turning toward the opposite wall. That's where he saw family photos. Well, he assumed they were family photos. In the pictures Holly stood next to an older man who looked remarkably like her. There was also a photo of Holly and the same older gentleman releasing what looked like butterflies into a sunrise.

"That was on what would have been my mother's fiftieth birthday. My dad and I wanted to do something special, so we released butterflies in her honor," Holly remarked, moving to stand right next to him.

"That's a wonderful way to honor someone," he said, thinking about his own father.

"We thought so too." Holly reached to pat Waffles on the head before she quickly turned away from him making her way over to the front door. She then toed off her black flats before slipping her feet into flip-flops that were placed by the door. She removed the elastic from her hair letting it fall naturally. The brief head shake she did to make her hair free rocketed right to his groin. *Oh, fuck!*

"Make yourself at home. I need to take Waffles out." She reached for his leash causing the little guy to jump around with excitement.

"Let me," Ben said before taking the leash from Holly's hand. "How about you set out some plates and put in the movie." Right now, he needed some distance from Holly. Whenever he was around her his body lost its mind and he forgot how to be a rational human being. He desperately needed some fresh air.

"You sure?" she asked, worrying her bottom lip. Yeah, he was sure... He needed to fight the urge to push her against the wall and nibble on that lip.

"You know where everything is and I'm sure us men can handle a little potty break." He bent to Waffles ruffling his neck before hooking his collar. "You gotta go potty, little guy?"

Waffles barked in excitement before jumping in circles causing Ben to laugh. "I'll take that as a yes."

Ben nearly ran Waffles out of the apartment and outside. As soon as the air hit his skin, he took a deep breath filling his lungs with the fresh Holly free air he needed.

The leash pulling on his hands brought him back to reality. He started walking Waffles around the front of the building waiting for him to do his business. "Did you know your mom is something else?" Ben asked, looking at Waffles who was on a mission to find the perfect spot.

"There's something about her that I can't put my finger on, but I can't get enough of it." Waffles ignored him as he found the spot he'd been looking for and started doing his business.

Once Waffles finished, he looked at Ben then back at the grass, then once again to Ben. "Damn. I guess Holly was right. You demand for it to be picked up right away." Ben barked out a quick laugh. "Well shit, you really do think of yourself as a King, now don't you?"

A few minutes later they returned to Holly's apartment. There were two plates set at the coffee table with two glasses of water.

Holly walked out of the kitchen with two dog bowls in her hands. "I saw you had Ripley's food in a little baggie, so I made her dinner too. I hope you don't mind I added chicken broth to it. When I was adding it to Waffles' food, Ripley looked at me like she was starved and started to whine."

Ben rolled his eyes. "Don't let her manipulate you, but yes, it's fine."

"I'm glad." She placed the food bowls at opposite ends of the living room before turning back to Ben. "You never know if there might be an altercation and I am pretty sure Ripley would kick Waffles' ass."

Ben's face brightened as he laughed. "You're probably right, and that's good animal parenting. I wish half of my clients were like you."

Holly smiled at him before she placed the Chinese food containers on the coffee table and sat down. "Everything is ready when you are." She grabbed her plate and started adding bits of food to it.

He sat beside her doing the same. "Did you put the movie in?" he asked, leaning back once his plate was full.

"Heck no!" Her eyebrows shot to the ceiling. "I do *not* do jumpy horror movies. Now serial killer, stabby movies, I'm fine with, but that crap you tried to pull, no way. Nope." She shook her head.

Ben couldn't help but smile. Even if his plan of scaring her into his arms didn't work out, her over-animated personality warmed him.

"Fine scaredy cat. What did you pick instead?" he asked, reaching for the remote.

"Some random comedy." Her eyes screamed with mischief as she placed a forkful of noodles into her mouth.

Ignoring it, he pressed play. A few minutes into the movie he groaned. "Grace, you've got to be kidding me, isn't this the vampire movie where they sparkle or some shit like that?"

Holly burst out laughing before grabbing the remote from Ben. "That's what you get for trying to scare me." Her face beamed as she maneuvered around the streaming program before picking a movie they would both enjoy. She placed the remote on the coffee table and started to eat again.

"You don't use chopsticks?" he asked.

"You've seen how clumsy I am, right? There is no way I'd get through a meal using chopsticks unscathed." She sat back on the sofa pulling her knees under her.

"You're right, Grace." He plopped a dumpling in his mouth with a chopstick smirking.

"Jerk." She jutted her chin toward the screen. "Watch the movie."

As the movie played in the background, Ben found himself inching closer to Holly's side of the couch. In his defense, Waffles and Ripley both joined them on the sofa pushing him closer to Holly.

He wasn't complaining, though. Instead, this gave him a better opportunity to watch her reactions. Holly became completely engrossed in the movie. She was on the edge of the cushion with her full attention on the screen. Her enjoyment in the scenes was contagious. Whenever there was a funny moment, she'd laugh as if she was the only one in the room. She had absolutely zero cares in the world.

His heart skipped.

Holly was genuine and in today's day and age that was a rarity. He focused his attention back to the movie and watched idly as he made sure to pet each of the dogs by his side that kept demanding his attention.

When the movie finally ended, he turned toward Holly. She glowed. The light reflecting from the screen illuminated her face, highlighting her features.

How the fuck was she so beautiful?

"Thank you for coming over," she whispered, staring at him. "It was a lot of fun."

"It was fun," he agreed. As the shadows danced on her lips, he saw the cut.

He watched as her tongue slipped out wetting her bottom lip. He couldn't hold back another second more. He leaned closer to her. When he heard her breath hitch, he whispered, "Holly..."

Her eyes widened as her breath quickened. He couldn't stop himself as he placed his hand behind her neck.

"Wh-what?" she stammered.

Ben looked into her eyes. "I'm going to kiss you."

CHAPTER EIGHT

THE AIR in the room thickened as Holly stared at Ben. Their lips only were millimeters apart from each other.

Could she kiss him? Her head felt light as she tried to analyze everything. Men like Ben were not supposed to want to kiss a frumpy, klutzy woman like her. Were they?

No.

Try telling that to Ben, though. Even in the darkness of the room Holly could see his eyes full of lust.

This was her do or die moment. Did she try to make sense why this Adonis wanted her or should she throw caution to the wind and go for it?

Even if he never spoke to her after tonight shouldn't she live her life? Or maybe she should live the life of the women she wanted to write about?

The sensual, sexy, confident women. The type of woman Holly always wanted to be. Plus, who was she to look a gift horse in the mouth?

That's it. She made her decision.

Throwing her arms behind Ben's neck, she launched herself into his arms. The moment her lips connected with his, the tension exploded. Throwing all her reservations aside, Holly kissed him like she was starved and his lips were her the only food she'd ever get again.

Ben welcomed every second of it as he wrapped his arm around her waist. He effortlessly leaned back onto the couch bringing her body on top of his, keeping her body molded to his.

Whoa Holly nearly choked on the thrill. She'd *never* be caught dead actually being on top of someone, but with Ben it was different. She wanted more.

She needed more. Thank fuck Ben must have read her mind again since his hands moved to her ass, squeezing it. He pulled her hips down as he thrust upward grinding their bodies together.

The friction rocked through her body sending earth-shattering sensations everywhere. She could already feel her slickness as Ben's member pushed against her apex.

"Fuck," he groaned, as he tore his lips from hers. "God damn, Holly." Ben moved toward her neck nibbling and sucking her skin.

"Not yet." Holly's breathy voice echoed through the room as she threw her head back giving him better access. She might not be super experienced in the lovemaking department, but she was well versed in her romance novels. Her mind raced to recall all of the information she'd read over the years that turned her on. And Ben kissing down her neck was one of them.

Ben's hand moved to her hips pushing her down harder onto his dick. "Fuck, I want you, Holly. I want you bad."

"Me too. Me too."

"Off." He grabbed the hem on her shirt pulling it from her body and throwing it behind him. Once she was topless, his hands moved to her lace covered breasts. "I knew you'd overfill my hands," he said more to her chest than her.

Mentally saying 'fuck it', Holly reached behind her unhooking her bra in one fell swoop. She tossed it behind her, doing her best to ignore the telltale sign of two dogs racing to play tug of war.

Ben's groan brought her attention back to him, though. He placed the palms of his hands on her back as he righted himself kissing down her exposed chest.

The moment he took her right nipple into his mouth, her nerve endings came alive. Ben's warm breath and whiskers were almost too much to handle.

"How are you this perfect?" he asked into her skin.

"Less talking, more sucking." She thrust her chest into his face which he gladly accepted. Ben's tongue circled her nipple before dragging it across her skin seeking out the other. He pulled that one into his mouth giving it the same treatment as the other.

Ben trailed his hands from her back to her legs wrapping them around his waist before moving her entirely onto her back. He started peppering hot kisses along her skin before making his way to her lips once more.

At least Holly wasn't the only one hungry.

She moved her hands to the hem of Ben's button-down shirt, letting her fingertips caress against his skin. Feeling his heat invigorated her. She could touch the bottom of his abs.

She wanted more.

She needed to count them. If this was her one shot at being with a Greek God, she might as well go for broke. She quickly thought back to a scene in a dark erotic novel she'd only finished a few days ago. With all the courage she could muster, she grabbed onto the bottom his shirt and pulled with all her might.

Nothing happened.

Not one button popped.

Holly opened her eyes to see Ben's amused face staring back at her.

At first she was mortified, but Ben's gentle kiss on the tip of her nose melted her heart. "Do you need some help, Grace?"

That name. Holly's eyes narrowed at him.

Before she could chastise him, though, he captured her lips with his. As she opened her mouth to say something his tongue slipped inside, making her forget her retort.

After a moment he pulled away and looked down at her. He straightened his back reaching for his shirt. Quickly he ripped his shirt open sending buttons flying across the room. "This is what you wanted, right?" That dang half smile appeared on his face as his eyes danced.

Holly was about to maim him for making fun of her, but the sight of his body made her lose all coherent thought. Was he always hiding such a perfect body under his clothes?

Holly touched his skin with her fingertips. When she caressed down his abs his muscles tightened, causing a hiss to escape from him.

Her index finger followed the dusting of hair that led toward his lower half.

Ben held perfectly still as he let Holly explore his body. Thank God, because right now she wanted to memorize every inch of him.

When Holly reached his belt, she looked into his eyes silently asking for permission.

With a slight nod from him, she brought both her hands to his belt. Taking a deep breath, she undid the buckle and unbuttoned his pants.

Quickly she pushed his pants and boxers down in one hurried move causing Ben's cock to break free nearly hitting her in the face.

"Holy McJeebers. How do you walk around with that thing?" Her eyes widened as she examined him. *This* was the kind of dick she'd only read about in her novels.

She looked at Ben's eyes once again only to see his amusement.

"Very carefully," he replied.

Holly looked back at his member and saw the tiny drop of moisture at the tip.

Could she? Hell yeah, she could. This was her one moment to shine. She quickly stuck out her tongue lapping at the bead.

When she heard him groan, she knew she'd done something right. When she went back to fully take him into her mouth, a hand fisting into her hair stopped her.

"Not this time, Grace. If you so much as look at my dick again I'm gonna explode all over your face."

Holly didn't see anything wrong with that. This was her ultimate fantasy come to life.

"Naughty girl," he remarked with a tsk. "This time I want to be inside of you when I come. We can talk about other options later."

This time?

There wasn't going to be anything other than a *this time*. This was a one-night stand.

Holly knew that. She wasn't stupid.

Ben would make an excuse to leave once they were done and she'd never hear from him again. She'd already resigned herself to accepting that.

She might as well enjoy every ounce of it she could.

However, before she could bring him back to her mouth, Ben scooped her into his arms effortlessly.

"Bedroom?"

Ben's skin was on fire and he loved every fucking second of it.

"I'm too heavy, you Neanderthal!" Holly screamed, clinging to his shoulders like she was going to fall.

"Are you calling me weak?" he asked, before nipping at the skin on her neck.

"Ouch. Jerk. No, I'm not calling you weak I'm trying to save your back."

He smacked her ass. "The next time you say it, I'll do it again, sweetheart. Tell me where your bedroom is." The same spot he smacked he then squeezed.

Holly's whole body tightened against him, as he squeezed harder. "The only other room in the apartment."

Ben looked around and saw one door. With his destination acquired he started toward the room. Unfortunately for him, he forgot about the two eager energetic dogs at his feet.

When he was only one foot from the bed, Waffles ran in between his legs.

"Shit!" Since Ben's pants were already half-way down his legs, he wasn't able to counter the obstacle. His only option was to toss Holly onto the bed, and fall down nearly onto of her.

"Hey! Gently. Whoa." Holly pushed her hair from her face.

"Blame Waffles." Ben tried to lift one of his legs onto the bed when he felt a tug.

When he looked he saw Lord Waffles attached to his jeans pulling.

Holly must have seen it too, because she burst out laughing. Waffles, Stop!" The dog didn't flinch. Instead he tugged harder.

Ben looked back at Holly who had tears in her eyes from laughing so hard. He couldn't help but laugh himself as he yanked the material from the dog before pulling them off and tossing them onto the Corgi's head. The little devil fought his jeans for a moment before taking them into the living room as if he'd won a prize.

An ear-to-ear grin appeared on his face as he looked back at Holly. "I knew sex with you would be entertaining."

Another laugh escaped Holly, making her breasts bounce. That had heat running through Ben again.

With his dick at attention, he pumped himself once. Twice. And as he was about to do it again, the room fell silent. As he looked into Holly's eyes, he knew his lust mirrored hers.

Then the devil bit her bottom lip causing a new wave of desire to wash over him. He crawled toward her on the bed. "You've got too many clothes on," he growled.

"Are you going to do something about it?"

Fuck yes, he was going to do something about it.

His eyes scanned her body. Her curves enticed him, and the roundness of her soft stomach made him want to kiss it. He let out a strangled breath as he placed his hands on her black pants and slowly started to bring them down her legs.

Once they were gone, he looked at her. Really looked at her. From her thick thighs all the way to her lust filled eyes.

He wanted her.

He wanted her so bad he could taste it.

Ben hooked his thumbs into her panties and slowly peeled them from her body leaving her completely naked.

Holy shit.

Holly was fucking beautiful.

As he watched her, he saw worry cloud her eyes. The moment she tried to hide herself with her hands, he gently held her arms down. "Shhh, let me show you."

Ben needed to make sure Holly understood how beautiful he thought she was.

Her body tensed as he moved his face toward her apex, inhaling deeply as her scent made his mouth water.

"Ben..." Worry clouded her voice.

"I've got you." Before Holly could protest further he used his shoulders to spread her thighs.

When he took his first taste, her flavor exploded on his tongue. *Fuck him.*

He'd tasted many women in his life but none were as sweet as Holly. He couldn't get enough.

Within seconds Holly's hands were at the back of his head pushing him deeper into her. There was something about a woman taking charge that drove him wild just as it did when she jumped him on the couch. He kept going until her legs snapped around his head and her body started to shake.

"Yes, oh yes. Don't stop."

Never.

Ben pulled her clit into his mouth lightly biting down. He was instantly rewarded with her moisture flooding his mouth.

That is how you satisfy a woman.

He pulled away from her core as Holly laid limp on the bed her chest rising rapidly as she tried to catch her breath.

He couldn't stop himself from licking his lips.

"Please tell me you have a condom?" Ben braced himself on his knees as he looked down at her.

Without opening her eyes, Holly lazily pointed to her nightstand.

He laughed as he leaned over her body opening the drawer.

Holy shit.

Ben's heart stopped the moment he saw her little collection of toys. Quickly, he made a mental note to remember they were there. They were definitely going to come out and play one day.

But, not today.

Pushing aside the images of Holly using them, he put the condom on and wrapped her legs around his waist. He then brought himself to her entrance.

"Grace, my Grace, are you ready for me?" he asked slowly inching his way inside of her.

There was a hint of fear in Holly's eyes, but there was also desire. She gave him a nod.

Ben looked down at their joining, trying his best to control himself. Her light dusting of brown hair ignited him. He loved she wasn't bare like most women these days. Instead, she was lightly trimmed.

Fucking perfect!

He watched closely as he inched his way inside of her center. Clearly, he was going too slow. When he reached the halfway point, Holly shocked the shit out of him by lifting her hips, helping to accommodate him.

"Fuck, you're huge," she groaned.

Damn that nearly unmanned him. Clenching his teeth, he closed his eyes trying to think of anything else other than the clumsy, outspoken, funny, beautiful woman beneath him.

Once Ben felt himself completely inside her, he stilled letting her adjust. Truth was he needed the few seconds to regroup himself. Her heat coupled with her tightness drove him to the brink.

"I'm ready," she announced, encouraging him to move.

Holy shit. This was perfect. He wanted to burn this imagine into his head for the rest of his life. The way Holly felt, the way she looked. Damn he never wanted to forget this. He'd never seen anyone more beautiful in his life.

He needed to get a grip. He looked at their connection. Slowly he removed himself only leaving the tip, before thrusting fully into her.

Ben's whole body tightened. He wanted to take this slow, build her next release, but she felt too hot, too tight, too perfect.

"Next time. Next time I'll go slow." Ben started thrusting harder and faster. Making sure to reach between them pinching her nub. When Holly began to shake he knew she was on the brink. He deepened his movements as he quickened his assault on her clit.

"Now. Holly. Fuckin' come now!"

He didn't have to wait for an audible response. Holly's walls tightened like a vise grip around him. She shot off the bed, as her second orgasm of the night took hold. He reached for her hips pulling them onto his dick, bringing them as close as possible. Holding her there he stilled, releasing himself.

His own orgasm shook through his body.

His breathing became ragged as sweat marred his body. He'd never felt this good being with someone before. Placing his hands around Holly's waist, he brought her on top of him. He then flipped them over so he was on his back. "Fucking perfect," he said.

Holly laid her head on his chest, her own breathing out of control. "I'd say." She started circling his nipple idly with her fingertip. "When I've read scenes like this in books I'd used to roll my eyes and say the author had an overactive imagination." Holly turned her head to look up at Ben. "Guess I was wrong?"

CHAPTER NINE

It'd been a total of three days since Holly heard from Ben. Looking at the clock on her desk she felt the familiar ache she'd grown accustomed to. Seventy-six hours twenty-five minutes and thirty-four seconds, to be more exact.

She shook her head. She didn't know why she cared, it's not like she didn't know this would be the outcome. Ben had been her once in a lifetime chance and she was happy she took it.

Holly pulled out her phone and looked at the screen. Nothing.

It still hurt, though.

She couldn't quite wrap her head around Ben leaving her high and dry. Especially, after the way he'd treated her throughout the night and the following morning.

This is what you get for dreaming...

After what Holly could only describe as the best sex of her life, he'd held her and softly caressed her skin for hours. Once she'd fallen asleep, he woke her with his expertly skilled head between her thighs. It wasn't just the sex, though.

Ben took care of her in the way you would a serious lover. He'd also surprised her by taking Waffles out, cooking a full-blown breakfast, and his goodbye kiss as he made his way off to work reeked of promises of what was yet to come.

You're such an idiot.

"Why the long face?" Mildred inquired, tearing Holly from her thoughts.

Damn it. Not now.

Holly did her best to keep her tears at bay. She hated feeling this vulnerable. It wasn't like she didn't know he wasn't really into her. She was a convenience for him. A horny man will always go for the easy option and that's what she was.

Nothing more.

Clearing her throat Holly looked at Mildred. "I don't have a long face." She winced when she heard the fakeness in her voice.

"Honey, I may be an old coot, but I can tell when a girl's gotten her heart broken. What did that hunk of burnin' love do? Want me to tear his balls off and make him eat them?"

There was a seriousness in Mildred's tone Holly had never heard before. "Mildred, you are something else." Holly laughed for the first time in days.

"I'm like a fairy godmother or something like that. Why don't you tell me what happened and I'll make it all better? Or if I can't I'll call in a favor and they will." Mildred winked.

"I don't know if I want any of your favors being connected to me in any way." Holly flipped her phone over checking to see if Ben had texted her.

Her shoulders dropped when there were no messages or calls. *Buck up, Holly. You had mind blowing sex with a sex god. Put that checkmark in the, "you are freakin' awesome" column and move on.*

Mildred placed her hand on Holly's arm drawing her attention. "Seriously, Holly, do you want to talk about it?"

Holly should talk about it, as soon as she spilled her guts she'd feel better right?

Screw it. "You know, Mildred, I have no idea what happened. But I am not going to let it get me down. If Ben wanted a quick roll in the hay, that's okay because I got some earth-shattering orgasms out of it. It doesn't matter to me if I haven't seen hide nor hair of him in three days." She looked at the clock on her desk. "Seventy-six hours thirty-two minutes and ten seconds. It doesn't bother me one bit."

"Sure, it doesn't," Mildred remarked, moving a hair back from Holly's crazy rant. "Men are pigs, honey. And in the end if you had yourself a good time, right on, and more power to you. However, if he physically hurt you or did something malicious let me at him."

"No. It wasn't anything like that. It was more of a, we started a friendship that could possibly turn out to be pretty cool, then we slept together and he left. That's it. Nothing more. Nothing less."

Mildred sat there for a few minutes observing her. "If it was nothing more than why are you bothered?" she asked, gently.

Why was she bothered? That was the million-dollar question. "It's not that I'm particularly bothered," she answered. "It's more of a, I knew this was going to happen, but it still stings, you know?"

Mildred nodded. "Well let's focus on something else." From the pocket of her long skirt Mildred pulled out the pen and pad she always carried with her. "Can you tell me more about the earth-shattering orgasms, please?"

Holly shifted back into her seat more and burst out laughing.

"You *are* something else, Mildred. That's why I love you."

"Aww, you love me?" She placed her hand on her chest. "Be still my heart. But honey, I have to tell you I'm a married woman, so you can't go using me as your rebound."

Holly rolled her eyes. "Damn. Well then, what's a girl to do?"

"If I were you, I'd march my butt to his front door and ask him what his problem is."

"I would never." Her eyes widened.

"Why not?" Mildred asked. "There is no rule that says a woman can't pursue a man. Even if she didn't want to pursue him, she could damn well ask him what his problem is."

"And have him laugh in my face? I think not."

"So, what if he laughs in your face? You can sock him right in the nose." Mildred threw her fist into the air.

Holly thought about it as Mildred pretended to fight the air. Could she really confront Ben? Would she want to?

"Here's the thing," Mildred continued. "I've known you for a while. I also know you overanalyze until your head explodes. You can either confront him and take the bull by the horns or you can sit here twiddling your thumbs until your mind has come up with a million different scenarios. All of which are probably wrong."

Holly leaned into the back of her chair. Mildred did have a point. If her past relationships or lack thereof told her anything, it would be she'd overanalyze every possible outcome or situation for days. But then again, she knew sleeping with Ben was probably a one-time deal. Why would she keep pushing it?

Mildred stood, putting her notepad and pen back into her pocket. "I think you should do it. Right now. You should get up from that chair and go confront him. His answer might not be one that you want, but in the end, you'll know. You'll be able to walk back in here with your head held high."

She was right.

"And, if it's really bad, I'll spend the next few hours in the Violent Crimes section getting pointers."

Holly couldn't help but laugh. Leave it to Mildred to go to the extreme. Outlandish as Mildred might be, she was right. This was Holly's chance to stand up for herself and all other women who've been wronged.

I am woman, so hear me roar.

Holly grabbed her purse and yelled to Mildred, "I'll be back in a little while. Cover for me."

"Always."

God Damnit!

Ben's nostrils flared as he did his best to rein in his emotions. Right now, he paced the exam room trying to stop himself from pulling out his own fucking hair.

"Benjamin, I don't understand why you refuse to give up this silly dream and work in your rightful place," his mother Barbra asked, crossing her arms over her chest.

"Why are you even here?" Ben stopped pacing and glared at her.

"To get you to do the right thing."

Ben mentally ordered himself to calm down. He'd spent the last two days up to his eyeballs in back to back emergency surgeries. Unfortunately, two dogs had been hit by cars within forty-five minutes of each other. Both operations took over six hours.

Then, when he thought he'd gotten a moment to catch his breath, he'd gotten a call from his buddy, Will, down at the police station. They'd saved a kitten that'd been poisoned by a local troublemaker. Thankfully, the police were able to catch the punk, but the poor kitten was in rough shape. At twelve weeks old, the poor guy's body didn't have the strength or ability to fight.

Ben spent the whole day trying to save the little guy.

As of right now though, because of Ben's quick actions, they were all on the road to recovery. But, he hadn't had a moment to himself. The few hours he'd slept were in the cot he kept in his office when he wanted to stay close to a critical patient. His phone died on day two and now to top off all of his frustrations, his bitch of a mother was here once again demanding that he take his rightful place at the head of Richman Industries.

Rightful place. Fuck off.

"I *am* doing the right thing," he snapped. *Take it easy,* he told himself. His mother thrived on confrontation.

"You think playing with these flea-ridden mangy *creatures* is the correct choice for you?"

Don't get angry. Don't get angry. "Yes, *mother*. This is the right choice for me."

As his mother opened her mouth to respond the exam room door flew open.

"Why have you been ignoring me?!" Holly stormed into the room with his receptionist Stacy, hot on her tail.

"I'm so sorry, Dr. Ben. She came in and refused to wait. When she heard your voice she ran in here," Stacy tried to explain.

"It's fine, Stacy. I'll take it from here." This was the last thing Ben wanted to deal with. Holly meeting his mother was something he wanted to avoid inevitably if he could.

"Who is this..." His mother looked Holly up and down. "Peasant?"

Holly's head shot toward his mother. "Who are you calling a peasant, you old hag?"

Holy shit. The fire coming from Holly made him hot.

"Excuse me, young lady?" His mother's eyebrows shot to the ceiling. "I do believe you did not refer to me as an old hag."

Holly mimicked his mother beautifully as she looked her up and down. "Actually, I did. But right now, this doesn't concern you." Holly turned her attention to Ben. Her eyes showing more fire than he'd ever seen. However, when he really looked at her, he saw pain if even just a small hint of it.

"Ben." He could see the panic and vulnerability in her.

"Young lady, you need to leave right now. I am having a private conversation with my son, and you are *not* invited."

Holly's eyes widened as her faced paled. "Oh, shit."

"Why am I not surprised a woman of your stature would also have a filthy mouth?" his mother remarked.

"Knock it off," Ben demanded, stepping in when he saw Holly physically swallow.

Barbra turned from Holly and stared at him for a moment before her eyes narrowed. "Benjamin, you have got to be kidding me. Have you really stooped so low as to associate yourself with this *woman?*" she asked, shaking her head. "Please tell me she isn't pregnant? I can't tell with all the weight around her middle."

"Knock it the fuck off, Barbra," Ben spat. From the

corner of his eye he could see Holly start to slowly back away toward the door.

He pointed at her. "Don't move." Turning back toward his mother, he glared. "Don't ever fucking say shit like that to or about Holly. So help me God, it will not end well for you."

"You admit you're sleeping with her then?" she asked, not even phased by Ben's words.

"We're not," Holly squeaked.

"Oh, thank God. I was worried he'd muddy our family with you." Barbra glanced at Holly.

"Get the fuck out!" Ben ordered. "By the way, I *am* sleeping with her and I will continue sleeping with her. I'll also make sure to come in her so many times she has no choice but to get knocked up."

His mother gasped before placing her hand on her chest. "I did not raise you like this."

"You didn't raise me at all."

"If your father were here he'd be ashamed of you."

Ben's eyes hardened as he clenched his teeth. "Do *not* bring dad into this."

"I'm only speaking the truth. He'd be so disappointed in you. First, you refuse to give up this silly play job and come work for Richman Industries, and now you're sleeping with *her.*"

"Stacy," Ben yelled, calling for his receptionist.

She came running into the room a moment later. "Yes?"

"Can you do me a favor and call the police station and ask for Will? I need him to remove my mother from the property." Stacy's eyes widened before shooting to his mother.

"Well of all things," Barbra said, she gathered her belongings in a huff. "I don't know what's gotten into you."

She turned her glare from Ben to Holly. "This is not acceptable behavior for a Richman. This is not the last time you'll be seeing me, Benjamin." She walked toward the door stopping in front of Holly. "And this will *not* be the last time I'll be seeing you either."

His mother stormed out of the exam room leaving him, Holly, and Stacy in her wake.

Taking a deep breath, Ben looked at his receptionist. "Can you do me a favor and hold my next appointment for a few minutes? I want to talk to Holly."

"No need to," Holly squeaked. "I'll see myself out."

"Don't move a muscle," he demanded, causing her to plant her feet on the ground.

"Sure thing, Doc." Stacy closed the door behind her leaving Holly and Ben alone.

Holly broke the awkward silence first. "I'm sorry for barging in here."

"Don't," he said, bracing himself on the exam table. The same exam table he'd placed Holly on the day they'd met. "I'm sorry you had the misfortune of meeting my mother."

"She seems wonderful," Holly scoffed.

"Sure, wonderful is a word you can use." He swiped a hand across his face before turning toward Holly. "Before we get into what just happened, I want to say sorry for not calling you."

"Don't worry about it. It hasn't even crossed my mind." Holly worried her bottom lip before straightening her chin.

"Is that so?" The corners of his mouth lifted.

She looked away briefly. "I thought about it once or twice."

"Then you only stormed in here to what?"

"Well, you see..." She looked around the room. "Okay, fine. You caught me. I wanted to know why you disappeared. I mean, I know I'm probably not the best lay." She looked away. "Before we slept together I thought we were, I don't know, starting some weird friendship or something. Plus, Waffles really likes you. I wanted to know what happened, so I can be honest with him when he demands for your presence." She shrugged.

Her vulnerability warmed him. It also made him realize he'd gotten under her skin just as much as she had gotten under his.

In two swift steps, Ben was in front of her. His fingers threaded through her hair as he devoured her mouth. He'd missed her lips the past three days. Once he had his fill, he pulled away from her, resting his forehead on hers. "I'm sorry," he said again. "I planned on calling you tonight and begging you to give me another chance."

When she opened her eyes he saw doubt there which killed him. "I'm serious. The day I left your apartment I had two separate dogs hit by cars."

She gasped.

"Then when I finally got that under control a friend at the police station brought in a kitten that had been poisoned. The only spare moments I had were spent sleeping on the cot in my office."

His eyes closed remembering the events of the last few days. He loved his job, but sometimes it took a toll on him.

"Did they all make it?" she whispered. When Ben opened his eyes, he saw the tears cascading down Holly's cheeks. Right then and there, he knew this was the woman for him. He used the pad of his thumb to wipe away the tears. "Would you like to meet them?"

She nodded.

Ben reached for her hand before pulling her into the back room and made their way over to the kennels. "This is

Murphy. He's been a long-time patient of mine. His leg got pretty messed up, but he'll be fine. I'm going to release him to his owners tomorrow."

Holly nodded, keeping silent. Ben could see the tears still in her eyes. "Over here is Red, a Blue Tick Beagle. He didn't fare as well. We had to fix quite a bit of internal bleeding, but he's on the up and up now. I'm going to keep him here a few more days, but I'm positive he will make a full recovery. His owners have been in every day to see him."

"That's wonderful," Holly whispered, never tearing her eyes from Red.

"Would you like to meet the kitten?"

"It made it?" Ben heard the hope in her voice.

"Yes, baby. He made it." Ben gently pulled her to one of the cages by the wall. Pointing to the one in front of them. "This is him. He's improved tenfold, but he still has a little twitch in his head. It's nothing I'm too concerned about. I've done everything I can to flush the poison from his body. His last blood test results showed all the poison is gone. He might have lasting neurological issues, though. I'm waiting to see if the twitch is going to be a permanent side effect or if it will fade in time." He put his fingers through the bars and the little orange and white kitten slowly moved to the bars rubbing them. He'd improved remarkably over the last day, Ben could even hear his purr through all the noise of the clinic.

"He's so friendly," Holly announced. "Can I pet him?"

"Sure thing, baby."

Holly placed her finger through the openings, and the kitten instantly started to play with her. "He's so cute."

Ben nodded. "Not as cute as you," he announced, with a cheesy grin which made Holly laugh.

"I see you've been busy."

"I have. Holly, I'm sorry for not calling you and telling you what was going on. After the first surgery I was going to text you, but I realized my phone died. I don't have my charger here. As soon as I got a free minute, I planned on running home to get it."

Holly relaxed as she played with the kitten. "It's okay, Ben."

"It's not. I don't want you thinking I did a hit and run. It wasn't like that for me." He placed his fingers under her chin making her look at him. "I want to date you."

Holly's breath hitched. She tried to mask it by moving her attention back to the kitten. "What happens to him once he's healed?" she asked.

Ben chuckled at her avoidance. Going back to the kitten himself he touched the bars. "I don't know. If he ends up with the twitch he'll be considered a special needs animal. Shelters won't take him. Then again, I haven't really thought about it. I want to keep him here as long as possible to make sure—"

"I want him," she interrupted. "I mean, I've taken care of cats before. I loved Princess Huffle Stuffle with my whole heart." She wiggled her fingers getting the kitten's attention. "Do you want to come home with me, Twitch?"

Ben's heart nearly exploded in his chest. The tenderness Holly had for animals was astonishing. It then clicked. "Did you just name him Twitch?"

"Yeah," she answered. "It's kinda fitting don't you think?"

Ben looked at her as a sweet smile appeared on his face. "Yeah, I think it is." He took the pen from his pocket and under the line that said owner on the paper hanging on the cage he wrote Holly. Along with Pet's name: Twitch.

He turned back toward Holly, her face beamed with excitement right before her eyes narrowed. "You're going to come in me so many times I have no choice but to get knocked up?"

"Uh, about that."

CHAPTER TEN

WAFFLES SAT in the back of Holly's car as she drove to her father, Henry's house. She knew bringing Waffles along would lessen the blow of not seeing her dad in a few days. Holly had made a habit of visiting him every three days, minimum, but with the recent events she was ashamed to admit it'd been almost five.

Turning into the driveway she glanced into the rearview mirror. "Waffles, get your nose out of the grocery bags!"

Waffles eyed her for a moment before he continued his quest.

"So help me God, Waffles. I will turn this car around and drop you off at home." Hoping Waffles wouldn't call her bluff, she waited for his response. After a standoff, he removed his head from the bags before plopping onto the seat.

"Good boy." Waffles wagged his butt, showing her he knew he was a good boy.

Holly parked the car in front of the garage as she did every time she saw her dad. She leaned back in her seat, looking at the two-story bungalow that she'd called home for so many years. The wear and tear was now clearly visible on the house. She could recall all the times her father would be on a ladder, installing new and improved windows, painting trim, or even fixing loose shingles.

Her father thrived on tinkering with the house. Every few years, he'd restain their front porch and he'd always let her help. Her father found his happiness working around the house.

That all came to an end one day three years ago.

Holly could still remember the phone call from the hospital. That was before the unknown blood clot in his neck migrated to his brain. It'd been a dark day in the Flanagan household.

After many surgeries and months in rehab, her dad regained some of his motor functions. Paralysis had set in on his left side, though. He only had about fifty-six percent use of his left arm and he was able to walk again.

She wouldn't have known what would happen if her father had been confined to a wheelchair. Even now, she could still see the frustration in his eyes when he'd have to sit or lay down. Going from being on a ladder eighty percent of his free time, to not being able to stand for long periods took a toll on him, as it would anyone. Not to mention, the guilt he still harbored about his bills.

After being released from rehab, the bills started coming in. With her father's new handicaps he wasn't able to go back to work. That left the financial strain on Holly's shoulders. Sure, there were times she'd want to rip her hair out, especially when she'd try and renegotiate interest or a payment and she'd ultimately end up nowhere.

She wouldn't trade it for the world. She had her dad, and that surpassed everything.

And if you were to ask Holly, she'd tell you her dad was

still perfect. She loved spending the extra time with him and she never minded helping him around the house or making sure he had meals ready to go, clean laundry in his dresser, and a spick and span house.

It was the least she could do.

Her father gave her everything she ever needed growing up, and after her mother died, he took on that role, too.

Being able to give back a quarter of what her dad gave her was what daughters were there for.

Holly glanced around the outside of the bungalow. It'd seen better days. Right now, the porch had a few loose boards sticking up and there was paint peeling off some of the walls.

She felt that familiar pang in her heart. One day she'd be able to pay off his bills and find enough money to hire a contractor to fix the house. She believed that with her whole heart.

In the meantime she'd spent however many hours it took, searching the internet for tutorials and doing her best to implement them.

"Is that my girl?"

Holly heard the porch door slam. She then saw her dad hobble out of the front door looking in her direction. Happiness erupted through her. Even with his limp and arm plastered to his side, and the left side of his face drooping slightly, he was still the most handsome man around.

Waffles started to whine from the back seat. "Is that your Grampa?" Holly opened the door. Waffles took her cue and scurried over the center console before jumping out of the car. The dog was on a mission.

"How could I forget you, your holiness?" Henry beamed before bending to pet Waffles as the dog started jumping around him in circles. His butt waggled as fast as he could get it.

"Hey Dad." Holly got out of the car. "How've you been?"

Her dad stood. "I've been better," he admitted, which worried her a little. Her dad's go to answer had always been 'never better.'

"That so?"

"Yeah," he replied. "I've been missing my little girl. Where've you been the past week?"

Holly felt guilt rush through her. "I'm sorry, Dad."

"I'm just giving you a hard time, Pumpkin." He held out his arms, the left not as wide as the right. "Come give your old man a hug." She hurried into his arms, squeezing him.

"Missed you, Pumpkin."

"Missed you too, Dad."

"Come on, let's get the bags inside and we can catch up," he said, giving her one last squeeze.

Holly pulled away from him. "Can you do me a favor and go feed Waffles? I'll get the bags while you do that."

His eyes narrowed briefly as he scrutinized her. "I know what you're doing, missy. Just because I'm an old fart doesn't mean you can pull one over on me."

"Whatever do you mean?" Holly batted her eyelashes.

"I'll let you do it this time, but only 'cause I spent most of the morning trying to change the lightbulbs in the den and now my body's screaming."

"You did what?!" She glared at her father.

"Holly Ann Flanagan. The day I can't change my own light bulb is a day you might as well take me out back and shoot me." He crossed his arms over his chest.

"Oh, for the love of all things, Dad. I didn't think you

85

couldn't change them. I just want to make sure you aren't putting too much strain on yourself. Next time just wait for me, okay?"

"Whatever," Henry grumbled before turning to open the front door. "Come on, Lord Waffles. I've got some extra pieces of steak I can add to your food."

Waffles hearing his favorite word 'food' ran past both of them and into the house. Holly couldn't see him, but if she knew Waffles, he would already be in the kitchen sitting on his hind legs begging. "Figures." She rolled her eyes.

Once all the bags were brought in and put away, and the laundry was in the wash, Holly sat with her father in the living room and pulled out a book. Waffles sat at her father's side wedged between the side of the recliner and her father's leg. He laid on his back as her dad idly scratched his belly.

"How was your week, Pumpkin?" he asked.

Holly put down her book and looked at her father. Should she tell him about Ben? How could she even try and explain it when she didn't understand it herself? Deciding on the safe route, she blurted, "I'm adopting a kitten."

"Well, I'll be. You are? What made you think to adopt a kitten?" He started to ruffle Waffles' fur. "This little guy not enough for you?"

"Waffles is more than enough. It just kinda fell into place, you know? There was a kitten who'd been poisoned by some jerk troublemaker." Seeing the worry in her father's eyes, she held up her hands. "He's going to be fine. At least I believe so, other than the twitch he now has in his head. No shelter will take him, so I volunteered."

"A twitch?" he asked before scratching his chin. "So, he's a little messed up, just like me."

It felt like a knife stab right through her heart. "You're not messed up, Dad."

Ignoring her, he continued, "How did you find out about the little guy with a twitch?"

"Well, Ben was showing me two dogs he'd operated on after they'd gotten hit by cars and then offered to show me the kitten he'd saved." The words were out of her mouth before she could stop them.

"Right there!" her dad exclaimed. "I knew it'd come out of your mouth sooner or later."

"What are you talking about?" She tried faking innocence.

"I knew there was something a little different about you." He held up his hands in surrender when she gave him a dirty look. "Not bad, just different. And now, I know it has to do with a boy."

"A boy. Really?" She rolled her eyes. "I'm not in high school anymore, Dad."

"Then it won't be a big deal when I tell you to bring him over this weekend for dinner."

Holly's face paled. She couldn't bring Ben to dinner. No way. They weren't even really dating. At least she didn't think they were. Sure, he said he *wanted* to date her, and they had slept together, but that wasn't *dating*.

The palms of her hands started to sweat. She could invite him to dinner. It's not like she wouldn't see him before Saturday to ask. Ben texted her earlier in the day saying he'd be over later tonight for dinner and a "movie." Plus, how could she invite him to meet her father after the encounter she had meeting his mother?

She shuddered.

Taking a calming breath, she spoke, "Umm, well Dad, see it's still really new." Then before she could stop herself, she word vomited all over her father. "It all started when I bent over to pick up Waffles... you know, when the Frisbee came screaming through the air and hit me right in the face. That's when I met Ben, he was the one playing with his dog, Ripley, when the Frisbee had a mind of its own and honed in on me. It hit me so hard it chipped my tooth." At her dad's worried expression, she quickly continued, "Before I knew it, Ben had me at his best friend's dental practice fixing me right up. He's a nice dentist, Dad. You'd like him. Talks a little too much, but still nice. I'm not sure what happened next, but Ben and I started hanging out. A lot. He's funny, sweet, and he's a veterinarian. I showed up at his practice to talk to him, that's when I found out about the two dogs and the kitten. Everything kinda clicked, you know? He's a great guy, and by far the best sex I've ever—"

"Whoa there." Her dad grimaced.

Holly hit her hand on her forehead. "When will I ever learn to just shut up?" To her dismay Waffles barked in agreement.

"I'm going to pretend I didn't hear that last part, Pumpkin, and we are going to back it up a second." Henry sat straighter in his recliner. "You say, he accidentally hit you with something, but did everything he could to fix your cracked tooth?"

"Chipped," she corrected. "His friend is a dentist. My smile was fixed the same day."

"Well, I'm glad to hear that. You've got a beautiful smile, Pumpkin."

"Thanks, Dad."

"He's a veterinarian, and he saved the kitten you're adopting?"

Holly nodded. "Yeah. It was touch and go there for a while, and Twitch will probably always have the lasting side effects of the poison, but yes, Ben saved his life."

Henry scratched his chin again. "How long have you known him?"

"The kitten? Only a day." At her father's glare, she continued, "A little less than a week." Embarrassment washed over her. *Good going, Holly. Now, you've gone and told your Dad you've slept with a guy you haven't even known a week.*

"He sounds like he's a good man. If he did all you said he did, then he's all right in my book." Her dad readjusted himself in his chair. "He shouldn't have a problem coming over Saturday to meet me. You know, the honorable thing to do after sleeping with my daughter."

At a loss for what to do next, she threw in the towel. "I'll ask him tonight when I see him. Okay?"

"It must be serious if you're seeing him again so soon." Henry studied her.

"Um, well, yeah, Waffles has taken a liking to him."

Her dad threw his head back and laughed. "I guess if he has the Waffles seal of approval then who am I to question?"

"Can we drop it, please?"

"Sure thing, Pumpkin. Although I do expect him to be here with you on Saturday."

"I'll ask him, okay?" she huffed, grabbing her book and throwing it into her bag. *Just wonderful.* Now, she'd need to either come up with an excuse her father would believe about Ben not coming or actually ask him. *Won-der-ful!* That was the last thing she wanted to do.

"Don't go convoluting one of your elaborate plans there, missy. I expect him to be here no later than five o'clock Saturday. I'll pull out the grill and he can help me cook."

"*Really?*" She shot her eyes to the ceiling. *Please give me strength.* Taking a deep breath, she looked at her father. "Okay Dad, we'll be here. I'll probably have him bring his dog along as well."

"The more, the merrier."

"I'm gonna take Waffles and head home, okay? Your clean laundry's been put away, and you've got meals ready. I'll call you tomorrow. Do you need anything before we leave?"

Her dad smiled. "No, Pumpkin. I've got everything I need. I'll see you and your gentleman friend at four-thirty Saturday."

Four-thirty? What happened to five!

"Yes, Dad." She kissed his cheek. "I love you."

"I love you, too." Waffles started to whine. "And, I love you too, Waffles." Her father's words had the little guy running and jumping in circles.

"I'll call you tomorrow, Dad."

Once Holly got into her car with Waffles safely in the back seat, she pulled out her phone and text Ben.

We need to talk.

She received a reply instantly from him.

Is everything okay, Holly?

How could she ask him this, especially over a text? *Bad idea, Holly.* Shaking her head, she drew in as much strength as she could before she hit reply.

Umm, yeah. We'll talk tonight.

His reply sent shivers down her spine.

I'll be at your apartment in twenty minutes.

She gulped.

CHAPTER ELEVEN

Ben sat outside of Holly's apartment building. His nerves were shot. Work had been another tough one. It always was when loss was involved. Then, after getting Holly's cryptic text, he couldn't stop himself from freaking out. He knew their relationship was still new, and she'd still had reservations about them.

He couldn't help but think the worst. Was she going to break up with him?

Ripley whined beside him. He scratched her behind the ear. "I know, girl. I'm nervous too." Ripley placed her head on Ben's lap. She always knew when he needed comfort.

Hearing a noise, he looked from Ripley to the sidewalk. That's where he saw Holly walking toward him.

Warmth washed over him in a way he'd grown accustomed to around her. She'd brought a sense of calm to him.

She walked toward her building with Waffles at her side. He could feel the nerves radiating off her. She gave him a small wave. When Waffles realized Ben was waiting there he jerked out of Holly's hand and ran right for him.

"Waffles!" Holly tried to grab for him.

Ben dropped to his knees catching the runaway pup as he jumped into his arms. "Hey, bud." Waffles plopped onto his back demanding belly rubs. High maintenance was an understatement.

"Bad, Waffles! Don't pull out of my hands."

Ben looked at Holly, her face scrunched as she watched him. His nerves once again got the better of him. "Is everything okay, babe?"

"Uh, yeah. I mean, no yeah. It's fine." She turned away from him.

No, everything was not fine.

Ben stood from the two dogs now playing at his feet. He reached for Holly's shoulders turning her to face him. "What's wrong?"

Holly's eyes held so many emotions. "Let's talk about it once we get inside."

Wanting to talk inside could be considered a good thing. If she wanted to end it she would have done it outside. There was something else really bothering her. He felt his need to protect her kick in. If someone had hurt her or if she was in trouble, he'd do anything to fix it. Seeing her like this, felt like a knife right in his chest. "Okay, babe."

He whistled for Ripley, knowing Waffles would follow suit. Reaching down, Ben picked up both of their leashes before making their way inside.

The elevator ride to Holly's floor by far, was the most intense feeling he'd ever encountered in his life, even though he'd dealt with his mother on multiple occasions. The tension also started to affect the dogs. Waffles paced uneasy, whereas Ripley sat at Holly's legs leaning into her trying to give her comfort.

Ben watched Holly from the corner of his eye. She was unnaturally quiet. She worried her hands while biting her bottom lip. Every time she winced at the pain, he fought the urge to reach out to her.

Ben was at a loss for what to do next. Right now, he hoped whatever had her mind racing they'd be able to work through it together.

When they finally made it inside of her apartment he turned to her, unable to hold off a moment longer. "Holly, please tell me what's bothering you." He used his hard voice, just as he did when he told her not to move in his office.

His desired effect on her took hold. She snapped around facing him.

Unfortunately for her, though, the quick uncontrolled movements riled the dogs. Waffles ran between her legs causing her to stumble. When she tried to catch herself, Ripley decided she wanted to help. Ripley ended up blocking Holly's attempt at grabbing the nearby wall.

Within seconds she was on the floor.

"Fuck, baby, are you okay?" Ben raced to her side.

Holly sat on her ass, blowing her hair out of her face. "This is just another day in my life," she said, before putting the palms of her hands onto the floor, pushing herself to stand. Ben seeing what she was doing, grabbed onto her hips righting her in seconds.

"How do you always lift me like I weigh nothing?" she asked.

"You do weigh nothing."

"Humph."

His eyes hardened. "Are you making fun of your weight?" he asked. "Any excuse you give me to redden your ass, I'll take."

Holly paled.

Ben's eyes lit as he laughed. "Lighten up, Grace." He leaned over kissing her nose while lightly swatting her butt.

"Hey!"

Ben walked away with a chuckle before sitting on her couch. Patting beside him he signaled both the pups. Once they were by his sides, he leaned back. "Spill."

Holly watched him for a second before breaking eye contact with him.

"I mean it, Grace. Something's got you all freaked out and if I were being honest, I'd say it has me a little worried too. What's got you on edge?"

Holly started pacing. "Fine. You know how I went to see my dad today?"

"Yeah."

Holly continued pacing not looking at him. "I did all the normal things I do for him. Cleaning, doing the laundry, making sure he has meals planned and ready. But, I guess I looked different or something." She stopped pacing and stared at him nervously.

"Okay."

Holly took a deep breath and blurted, "He's demanding to meet you this Saturday for a cookout!" She started pacing again. "You'd be the one to have to cook on the grill, he can't really do that anymore. I told him I'd think about asking you, but he demanded you come. Especially, after I let it slip you were the best sex of my life. He said the manly thing to do would be for you to meet him, because you've already gotten the goods."

Ben's eyes widened for a brief second before he threw his head back in laughter.

"Don't laugh at me!"

Ben shot from his seat and in two steps landed in front

of her. "How can I not, baby? You're adorable." He kissed her.

When they finally came up for air, Holly panted. "What was that for? I mean I'm not complaining. I just thought after I told you you'd have to meet my dad, you'd be pissed."

He rested his forehead on hers. "Why would I be pissed, Grace?"

"It's a big step meeting my dad."

"Why?"

"I don't know, isn't it always a big step meeting the parents? We don't even know what we are yet."

He growled. "I know what we are, Holly." He lifted her into the air, wrapping her legs around his waist. "I'm the man that gives you the best sex of your life."

Holly placed her head in the crook of his neck. "You heard that?"

"You damn well better believe I did." He hurried them to her bedroom. Once he made it to the bed, he gently threw her on top of it, following suit. "We can talk about meeting your dad later. Which I have no problem with, by the way. It'll be nice to meet him. Right now, though, I want to expand on the best sex of your life."

Ben gazed down at Holly as she laid on the bed, her hair a ruffled mess. She never looked more attractive. He used his right hand and gently caressed her skin. "You're so beautiful," he murmured before he leaned down to pepper kisses on her neck.

"Enough talking, more doing." She squirmed.

"So feisty, Grace. I love it." Ben reached for the hem of her shirt forcing her to sit up as he removed it. His hands instantly went to her breasts as he started to massage them.

"They feel so good," he explained as he tweaked her nipple through her bra.

"What about you?" she asked, reaching for his shirt.

"Anything you want, baby." He reluctantly removed his hands from her breasts before ripping his shirt off and throwing it behind him.

"I still can't get over your abs." Holly reached for them and began to massage them. "Seriously, how is it possible that you look this good?"

"I have to keep up my strength. Do you know how hard it is to control a one hundred and twenty-pound Rottweiler who is nothing but muscle? It's not an easy task, baby."

Moving her hands south she started to unbuckle his jeans. Letting her right hand migrate a little lower she cupped him causing a hiss to escape from his mouth. "More," he pleaded.

"My pleasure." She used her hands and pushed against his chest causing him to fall backwards on to the bed.

A dominant woman is a wild woman, he thought before letting Holly take control.

His eyes were heavy-lidded with pleasure as he watched her crawl along his body massaging his muscles. "You wouldn't let me do this last time," she stated, leaning over his aching member. "I want to taste you properly."

Ben clenched his teeth as a moan escaped him, causing him to fist his hands at his side as he desperately tried to keep control.

Holly slowly lowered the zipper of his jeans before quickly removing the material from his body.

Ben's dick instantly sprang free glistening at the tip.

"Yes," she hissed. She grabbed onto the base, giving it a slight squeeze. "It amazes me you walk around with this thing. How do you not sit on it?"

He was about to give her a smart aleck reply when she enveloped him in her mouth.

"Oh fuck." Losing control of his hands, he fisted her hair.

Holly started moving up and down his shaft, swallowing once he was entirely inside of her mouth. "Don't do that," he growled.

She released him with a pop. "Why not?" Her eyes held a hint of worry. "Did I not do it right?"

"You did it too right," he growled, trying to keep his control.

"Oh." She smiled. "Okay then." Ignoring his plea, she went back to the task at hand. This time, she let her tongue dance across the head before sucking him in.

"Nope." He pushed her off before collapsing on top of her. "When I come, I want it to be inside of you."

"I was having fun." Her adorable pout made him smirk.

"Believe me, so was I. But I want you, Grace. I need to be inside of you." He moved down her body removing her pants and panties in one motion. "Don't you want that, too?"

She cocked her head to the side. "Well, duh."

"Exactly." With Holly's pants removed he let her legs fall open along either side of him. Looking at her core, her wetness called to him. "Plus, I intend to not make a liar out of you."

"What?" She gasped as he pinched her clit.

"I have to deliver on the best sex of your life."

Her eyes shot to him. "Oh, for the love of... are you ever gonna let me live that down?"

"Not on your life." He thrust himself inside of Holly, her walls instantly tightening around him as her orgasm rocketed her off the bed.

"Holy crappolie."

Ben pulled her into his arms so they were both sitting up. Holly's legs wrapped around him, as she sat in his lap, his dick fully inside of her. "Holy something is right." He used gravity to his advantage as Holly clung to him. His movements were deep and slow. He wanted to build her to another release.

Holly was always so damn responsive, she'd explode at the mere touch of his hand. Not this time, though. No, this time he wanted to build a slow burn inside of her. He wanted to mark her. He wanted her to remember what he felt like sunk deep into her, for days to come.

"Faster," she pleaded, clinging to him.

"No." Ben placed his hands on the small of her back forcing her to stop her bouncing.

"Please."

Grabbing the side of her hips, Ben slowly moved her in circular motions. He knew the friction along her clit would only intensify her pleasure. Holly began to shake as her breathing increased. Before she could come he flipped their position on the bed.

"No," she begged, trying to replace the sensation on her clit. "Please."

Ignoring her, Ben positioned himself behind her on his side. He wanted to feel every part of her skin and he knew the only way to do that was to spoon her. Throwing her leg over his hip, he gently thrust himself into her warm treasure. Using his left hand, he reached around them seeking out her clit.

"Oh God, Ben," she moaned.

He moved inside of her, feeling her walls clench around him. Pushing Holly's hair to one side, he whispered in her ear, "Now." He bit gently on her earlobe causing her to explode.

Holly's body convulsed around him caused his own control to slip. Ben stilled spilling everything he had deep within her walls.

"Holy crap." Holly tucked herself into his arms.

After only a few moments Ben heard Holly's gentle breathing and he knew she'd fallen asleep. He couldn't blame her.

Ben laid there with Holly curled in his arms.

This is how he wanted to spend the rest of his life. A huge smile spread across his face. Even though his body was exhausted, he couldn't fall asleep. His mind was too energized with the woman in his arms.

Ben thought back to their conversation. Her frazzled behavior about telling him her dad wanted to meet him was adorable.

"I have no problem meeting your dad, baby," he whispered making sure not to wake her. Ben kissed her temple before repositioning himself.

That's when he realized his mistake.

"Oh fuck." He looked at his soft dick with no condom on it.

Shit! His stomach bottomed out. How was he going to tell Holly he fucked up? Sure, he joked about knocking her up, and the more he thought about it the more he liked the idea. But, he would never force her into anything. "Fuck!" he groaned, pulling away from her.

"What?" Holly shifted to face him. "What's wrong?"

Ben jumped from the bed before pacing her small room. *Okay, it was one mistake it's not a big deal. She won't hate you.*

Waffles ran into the room, Ripley right behind him before they started to wrestle.

"Ben, you're kinda freaking me out here."

Ben stopped pacing long enough to throw his boxers out of the room making the dogs chase after them. He shut the door, locking them out before turning back to Holly. "I fucked up."

Holly reached for the comforter to cover her body, alarming him on how his words sounded. He snagged the material yanking it from her hands. "No, that's not what I meant."

Clearly not willing to believe him, Holly used her hands to cover herself. "What's the problem then?"

Ben crawled up the bed before cupping her cheeks in his hands and passionately kissing her. Pulling away he sighed. "There is something about you that carries me away. "

"Okay." She worried her lip.

"I forgot to put on a condom."

Holly's eyes widened before she looked between her legs.

Leave it to Holly to go there. Even in tension, she still found a way to make him laugh.

"Oh, umm, well I guess you're right." She looked at him.

"I'm sorry, babe. I would never willingly put you in danger."

"Do you have something?" Her eyes widened.

"No!" Ben reached for her hand squeezing it. "Hell no, I don't have anything. Shit Holly, before you, I hadn't had sex in almost a year."

"Almost a *year*?"

"Yeah. Don't look at me like that. I devote my time to my practice."

Holly sat on the bed not saying anything for a few minutes. "I'm clean too," she whispered. "The last time I had sex was way over a year ago, more like two."

Ben looked at her. "I know you're still worried about everything, especially, getting pregnant. I promise, Holly, I will be there for you no matter what. I've always wanted children—"

She held up her hands. "Holy crap on a cracker. I won't get pregnant. I'm on the pill, Ben. I have been for years."

Ben felt a weird sense of relief along with disappointment run through him. "Okay, what were you upset about?" He didn't like the idea there was no chance of her getting pregnant.

"I didn't want you to judge me that it's been way longer for me in the sex department."

"I wouldn't judge you," he assured her.

"Well, you make fun of me for other stuff why not this?"

He growled before jumping on her causing Holly to laugh. "I like the idea of knowing you haven't been with a lot of men. Makes me want you more."

"Whatever." She laughed before moving her neck to give Ben better access.

"It drives me wild."

"Well, I'm glad my lack of sexy times does it for you."

"It won't be lacking anymore." He nibbled on her neck.

"Good."

Ben made his way down her chest. He was about to suck her nipple into his mouth when he heard her laugh. He looked at her as she was trying her best to hold in her amusement. "Am I funny now?"

"No." She laughed. "I was just thinking about how you might have had to meet my dad knowing there was a possibility you'd knocked me up."

CHAPTER TWELVE

Holly parked the car in front of the garage at her father's house, like she did every time she visited. Only this time, the tension in her stomach made her want to throw up. Hoping Ben wasn't a mess like her, she looked out of the corner of her eye.

When she saw Ben sitting in the passenger seat with a stupid smirk on his face her eye started to twitch. *How is it possible he's this calm?*

"If you hold the steering wheel any tighter, you'll lose feeling." Ben laughed, jarring her from her irritation.

Holly quickly removed her hands from the wheel and placed them in her lap wringing them. "I wasn't holding it tight."

"Yes, you were, Grace." He cupped her chin with his left hand moving her head to face him. "It's going to be okay." He kissed her on the tip of her nose before kissing her lips softly.

"I know." Did she, though? This moment felt more real to her than anything she'd ever experienced in her life.

"I want to meet your dad, babe. Anyone that can help produce half of you must be pretty remarkable."

"Eww. Gross, Ben." She blanched before punching his shoulder.

"What'd I say?"

Waffles started to whine from the back seat scratching at the window, breaking up their conversation.

"Do I need to get the hose and cool you two off?"

Holly's head snapped around. Her father had come out of the house and now stood on the front porch staring at them.

"Oh, crap." Holly's eyes widened. Waffles barked doing everything he could to get out of the car and see his grandpa.

Ben laughed before opening his door for the little guy. Waffles jumped over the seat and ran past him, Ripley not far behind.

Ben exited the car and strode right to her father with his hand out. "Nice to meet you, Mr. Flanagan."

"Were you in there foolin' around with my little girl?" Her father nodded his head toward the car.

Oh, shit. Holly wanted the ground to open and swallow her whole.

"Depends on what your definition of foolin' around is?" Ben countered.

Her father analyzed him for a split second before roaring with laughter. "Call me Henry." He clasped his good hand on the back of Ben's shoulder. "I like you." Her dad looked at Holly and pointed at Ben. "We'll keep him."

"Kill me now," she grumbled before opening the car door. She made her way up the front steps trying her best not to die of mortification.

"This is Ben, Dad." She gestured toward him.

Henry leaned in kissing Holly on the cheek. "I figured as much, Pumpkin. I didn't think you'd bring another boy over." He bent at his waist. "And who's this?"

"That's Ripley. She's my Australian Shepherd," Ben replied, reaching his hand down to scratch the pup.

Henry's eyes hardened. "This the one you were playing with when you caused my girl to break her tooth?"

"Chipped, Dad. Chipped."

"Same difference." Henry crossed his arms over his chest the best he could before narrowing his eyes at Ben.

"No, it's not." Mimicking his movements, Holly crossed her arms over her chest. Was her dad trying to be difficult?

"Yes, sir. Unfortunately, the Frisbee had a mind of its own," Ben answered.

"But you got her all fixed up, though?"

"Yes, sir. It was my number one priority."

Her dad looked him up and down, trying to find the lie.

"Not sir. Henry. Sir makes me feel old."

"All right then, Henry. Making sure Holly was okay was all that mattered to me." Ben joined the party by crossing his arms over his chest.

"You sure it wasn't getting into her pants?"

Holly blanched. "Okay, that's enough." Holly pushed past the two opening the front door. "Everyone inside. Time to cook food."

Ben not moving a muscle stared her father in the eyes. "I think your daughter is the most beautiful woman I have ever laid eyes on. I'd be lying if I said I wasn't attracted to her, but no. I did not *only* want to get in her pants. It was *my* rogue dog toy that hit her making it my responsibility to fix whatever needed to be fixed. At that time, getting into her pants was not a priority; her health and safety were."

Her dad straightened. "And now?"

"Now, her health and safety are still my number one priority." Ben turned to face Holly who'd stopped in the doorway to witness the testosterone showdown. "Along with getting into her pants." He winked.

Holly's cheeks heated as she threw her hands in the air. "That's it." She turned away from them darting into the house making sure the door slammed behind her.

Holly heard both of them laugh before following her through the door.

"You've got moxie, and I like that," Henry remarked. "Holly needs someone like you around."

"I'm glad you think so. I plan on sticking around."

Holly hearing enough of their chatter grabbed the bag of charcoal that sat along the wall. "I'm going to start the grill."

"Are you leaving in hopes that we stop talking about you?" her father asked.

"No, I'm leaving because if I stay here any longer I'm liable to kill both of you."

"Feisty," Ben laughed.

"Isn't she?" Henry agreed.

Ignoring both of them, she picked up the bag and headed toward the back door. "Waffles, Ripley. Outside," she hollered over her shoulder.

"Now, she's even taking the pups." Henry pouted.

As Holly turned back to argue with him her foot snagged on the trim under the door. Before she knew it, she was falling to the ground. She braced herself for impact but it never came.

Opening one of her eyes, Holly realized she'd somehow ended up in Ben's arms instead of on the ground. "I can't take you anywhere, Grace."

"Holly, I'm so sorry." Henry ran over to her. "I forgot to

mention the door trim started coming up. I meant to get down there and nail it back but I couldn't get a solid grip on the nails," her father pleaded.

"It's okay, Dad," she tried reassuring him. "I'm okay."

"No, Holly, it's not okay. I meant to warn you about it." The disgrace in her dad's voice broke her heart in two.

"No harm, no foul," Ben said righting Holly. "Grace didn't even drop the bag of charcoal."

Her father straightened, before squinting his eyes. "Grace?"

"Holly's other name." Ben took the charcoal bag from Holly's hands placing it on the back porch.

"Is that some weird sex thing?" Henry asked.

"Oh God." Holly briefly closed her eyes.

"No," Ben laughed. "Holly's extremely graceful."

Henry nodded, with his own chuckle. "Ahh, now I understand. She is quite graceful, isn't she?"

"Very." Ben's eyes lit.

Henry turned to Holly. "I am sorry, Pumpkin."

"No worries, Dad. Everything is fine." Holly walked into his harms.

"Love you, Pumpkin."

"Love you too, Dad."

Two hours later, Ben had fixed the door trim and the food had been cooked and served. After their initial pissing war, everything between Ben and Henry seemed right as rain.

Actually, it seemed better than that.

Henry reminded him a lot of his own father. Within a short time, he'd felt the same level of comfort he'd had when his dad was alive. The two freely talked about everything from sports, animals, his condition, and Holly.

Ben loved the way Henry spoke about Holly. Ben could clearly see the love he had for his daughter.

Henry was a down to earth, blue collar man, and he admired that about him.

Ben could feel the pain coming from Henry when he talked about the joy he used to have fixing up the house. One look in his eyes and you'd see Henry thought he was less of a man now.

It broke his heart, even though he'd only met Henry now, he would help him anyway he needed. He would have done the same thing for his father if he'd been alive and in Henry's condition.

As Holly played with Ripley and Waffles in the back yard, Ben sat on the back porch listening to Henry. His eyes couldn't help but follow Holly as she ran through the yard tossing the tennis ball through the air.

For a split second, Ben replaced the dogs with their children.

"You've got it bad."

Henry's voice jolted Ben out of his fantasy. Looking at her dad, he shrugged, why deny it. "I do."

Henry sat back in the rocking chair.

Before Ben knew it, he started spilling his guts. "There is something about Holly that makes me want it all. I know that sounds insane, even more so that we haven't known each other very long, but I can't help it." He focused his attention on Holly.

"It's not insane, son."

Son.

Ben froze. Hearing that word caused a new pang of hurt

to rip through him. His dad used to call him son. Doing his best to ignore it, Ben looked at Henry.

"I felt that way about Holly's mother, Helen, when I met her." Henry got a faraway look in his eyes. "She took my breath away. I never could quite put my finger on it, but there was something about her that drew me in. It was like she was my homing beacon. We were married not long after we met."

Ben's eyes went back to Holly playing with the dogs as he listened to Henry.

"She was taken from me too soon."

Ben understood that. He felt the same way about his father. "I'm sorry."

"Don't be. Even though I ache for her every day. I would rather that, then not have had her at all."

"That's pretty deep." He looked back at Henry who was staring him down.

"Love is deep, son."

Ben lowered his head. *Yeah, it is.*

"Holly doesn't remember her mother as much as I'd like her to. I made sure I always brought up stories with her, and pictures to try and help her. She's a lot like her mother. Even acquired the clumsy gene."

Ben chuckled. "So, she does get it from somewhere?"

"Most definitely." Henry eyed him. "Helen was known for her clumsiness. I can't count the number of times I'd be talking to her at eye level and the next minute she was on the floor after stumbling over an invisible rock."

Ben snorted. "Sounds exactly like Grace."

"It was adorable."

Ben sat back watching Holly again. "It is. It makes me want her more."

Both men sat in silence for a few minutes before Henry

decided to speak. "You never know how long you're lucky enough to have someone," he whispered. "My only advice I can give to anyone is don't wait around. Take that leap and follow your impulse. We are all living by a time clock and no one knows when that clock stops."

Ben listened to the words and let them sink in. After last night's condom scare, he thought he'd be more on edge, more cautious. Even more reserved about settling down. The exact way he'd always thought when it came to his future.

Instead, he found himself following Holly in the backyard. His mind instantly pictured her swollen with their child. That image ignited something inside of him. Something he'd never realized he wanted.

"Food for thought," Henry remarked.

Ben watched as Ripley jumped onto Holly and stole the ball out of her hands.

"Get back here!" she hollered, running after Ripley. Waffles with his little legs ran alongside Holly trying to herd her just as Corgi's do, causing her to stumble in her steps.

Ben didn't know if it was too soon or not, but he knew for damn sure he was starting to fall in love with Holly. Hell, he might already be there.

"Go get your girl," Henry mumbled. "Seems as though she needs a little help." He jutted his chin toward Holly in the yard.

Ben jumped from his seat hopping down the steps to help steal back the tennis ball. "I plan on it."

CHAPTER THIRTEEN

HOLLY MANEUVERED her way around the endless book-shelves, trying to avoid Mildred's prying eyes. And so far, she'd done a pretty good job of it.

Placing a book in its rightful spot, she turned to her cart ready to grab the next book.

"Holy crap!" Holly held her chest trying to get her breathing under control.

Mildred stood next to the cart with her arms crossed over her chest. "Are you done avoiding me?" she asked, raising her right brow.

"I wasn't avoiding you."

"Liar! Now tell me everything." Mildred took the foot-stool at Holly's feet and sat.

After a few second standoff, Holly blew out a deep breath. "I don't even know where to begin."

"I'd say Friday night after you left is a good place to start." Mildred took her pad and pen out of her pocket, as she always did when gossip was involved. Crossing her legs, she readied herself to take notes.

"You're something else." The corner of Holly's lip turned up.

"Never said I wasn't."

Forty-five minutes and an inquisition later, Holly was back at her desk cataloging overdue books. Mildred was off in the romance section scouring to find tips. For who? Holly didn't know, but it was best to leave Mildred to her research when she was on one of her kicks.

"It wasn't hard to find you."

Holly looked from her task to see Ben's mother Barbra walking toward her.

Wonderful.

"Hello, Mrs. Richman. Can I help you find anything?" Holly placed a smile on her face and did her best not to scowl at the woman.

Barbra marched toward her like she had a stick up her ass. At this point, Holly wouldn't have expected anything else. "No." Barbra sized her up. "You cannot help me find anything. What I *need* you to do is stay away from my son."

Holly recoiled in shock which instantly melted into anger. Who the hell did this bitch think she was? "I'm sorry, Mrs. Richman, but that's not something I am willing to do." She squared her shoulders.

"It's money you're after, isn't it?" Barbra reached into her purse ignoring Holly's now stunned expression.

Holly's body shook with anger. Crossing her arms over her chest, she raised her brow in challenge. "Excuse me?"

"You heard me, young lady." Barbra closed her purse in a huff, before looking down at Holly. "Are you only with *my* Benjamin because he has money?"

That sealed the deal. Yes, this bitch was crazy. "First off, *old* lady, I am not *only* with your son because he has money. I didn't know he had money when I first met him."

Barbra narrowed her eyes. "Likely story."

"What's your freakin' deal?"

"My deal?" Barbra asked. "I'll tell you what my deal is. I cannot have my Benjamin be seen with the likes of you. You'd only ruin the reputation he's worked so hard to achieve. If word gets out he's with someone like *you*, all my hard work would be for nothing."

Holly shook her head in disbelief. "Wow. Some mother you are."

"I am the *best* mother. I'd do anything I can to protect his name."

"You mean your name."

Opening her bag once again, Barbra removed her checkbook. "I am here to offer you ten thousand dollars to stay away from my son."

Holly's mouth fell open while her eyebrows shot to the ceiling. "Are you kidding me?"

"I do not kid."

"Wow." Holly sat back in utter disbelief. "If you're not joking then you are seriously messed up in the head. You can't buy me, *Barbra*."

"Everyone has their price," she stated matter of fact. "And, I just so happen to know yours."

"Listen here, you crazy whack-a-doo, I will never take a dime from you."

Barbra placed her checkbook back in her bag. "Are you sure about that?" she sneered. "I know your father's medical bills are piling up. I also know if you don't pay his back mortgage by the end of the month, his precious little home will be set for foreclosure."

All of the blood drained from Holly's face. "How did you know that?"

"I own this town, *Holly Flanagan*. I know everything."

Holly stared at her as her heart froze in her chest. Could Ben's mother honestly be this evil? Taking a deep breath, Holly squared her jaw. "I don't appreciate you going through my father's financial records."

Barbra's eyes lit as she chuckled. "Do you think my regard for others got me to where I am now?"

"You mean a coldhearted bitch? No."

"Glad you think so." Barbra turned on her heel before looking over her shoulder. "I wonder if you understand four out of the five members of the library's board of directors are personal friends of mine. I do hope you hadn't had your heart set on working here much longer."

"Excuse me?" Holly's eyes widened.

Barbara turned back. "You heard me, you little whore. Maybe I should say *big* whore. Stay away from Benjamin. You're not what he needs, and you'll never be good enough for him. You're nothing but a poor unfortunate excuse for a human being. Mark my words, Holly Flanagan, if I so much as hear you've been seen with Benjamin..." She stopped talking while a creepy smile spread across her face. "All it takes is one phone call and you can say goodbye to your precious little job. Hmm, I wonder what will happen to your poor disabled father? There's no way you'd be able to pay all his bills." She placed her finger on her chin looking at the ceiling. "Oh, well."

"You wouldn't?"

Barbra laughed. "You don't think I will?" Her expression hardened. "Hear this missy, I will do anything I need to protect my son from the likes of you. I have no problem destroying your life and the life of your poor sad sack of a father if I need to." Without another word she turned on her heel and marched out of the library.

Holly sat there frozen as the implications of Barbra's

words swam around her head as her heart raced.

How could there be someone so awful like Barbra? Panic started to creep in. She looked at the picture of her father on her desk.

Her dad meant the world to her. In every way, shape, or form. She'd never do anything that could potentially hurt him in any way.

What if Barbra followed through on her threats? If Holly lost her job there would be no way she could pay her father's bills and keep him out of a nursing home.

She couldn't fail him.

She wouldn't fail him.

"What a bitch." Mildred walked from behind a book-shelf. "What crawled up her ass?"

Holly couldn't speak not while everything was falling apart.

Even though she still couldn't help having doubts about Ben, she foolishly thought she was on the right path for once. But now, with even the mere thought of her father suffering, caused bile to rise in her throat.

Panic set in. This couldn't be happening.

"Holly, honey, are you okay? You've lost all the color in your face."

Snapping out of her trance, Holly looked at Mildred with tears pooling in her eyes. "She demanded I stop seeing her son and if I don't she'll have me fired." Holly's heart was on the verge of exploding from her chest. "I can't lose my job, Mildred. More than half of my paycheck goes to my dad. If I lose my job, *he'll* lose everything."

Mildred placed her hand on Holly's shoulder. "Calm down, honey. I am sure we can come up with a solution. One where you don't lose your job, and you can still see that sexy man meat."

"What solution? You heard her. She owns this town. She could destroy me and my dad in one phone call." Holly held her hand against her stomach willing the bile to stay down.

"I understand you're panicking right now, and I would be too," Mildred calmly replied. "I think you should call Ben and talk to him."

Holly jerked out of Mildred's grasp. "Call Ben? Did you hear what just happened? I can't call Ben. If she finds out it'll all be over." Holly grabbed her purse and ran toward the door.

Once she made it outside, she looked down the street. Her first instinct was to run to Ben's clinic and into his arms. As she took her first step her phone rang so she blindly answered. "Hello?"

"Hi, Pumpkin," her father's voice came over the line.

"Dad."

"Holly, I wanted to know if you were coming over tonight? I got a strange call from the bank and wanted to talk to you about it." Holly's heart shattered into a million pieces as she clenched the phone to her ear. She looked down the street toward the direction of the clinic. She knew she had a choice.

She swallowed before closing her eyes, allowing a stray tear to slide down her cheek.

Holly could go to her father, the man who raised her and had been there forever through everything in her life. The father, who'd become her best friend. The father she owed her life to. Or, she could run to the man who she knew she'd already fallen in love with.

As the tears freely cascaded down her cheeks, she already knew the answer.

CHAPTER FOURTEEN

BEN PLACED his hammer on the ground before wiping the sweat from his brow. He'd spent the better part of the morning replacing wood on Henry's porch, and the sun's heat made sure to make its presence known.

Henry was a good man. Ben could see why Holly loved him so much.

That's why on Sunday, he personally called all his scheduled clients and rearranged them throughout the week leaving his Monday completely free. Thankfully, his clients were more than happy about the "inconvenience" if it meant they'd get free service when they did come in for their appointment. He did however make it clear if an emergency arose, he'd be at the clinic in a heartbeat.

Ben wasn't quite sure what compelled him to show up at Henry's doorstep at seven in the morning, but he knew after Holly's near accident over the weekend and the look of devastation that ran across Henry's face, he knew he wanted to help.

Glancing around the porch, he felt the corners of his mouth turn upwards. Over the watchful eyes of one Henry

Flanagan, the porch was looking ten times better, if he did say so himself.

Ben chuckled when he saw Ripley sprawled out on her back in the shade, doing her best to keep herself cool.

"I brought you some water," Henry announced, handing the glass to Ben with his good hand.

Thankful for the gesture Ben gladly took the glass. "Thanks." Taking a huge swig, he let the cold water slide down his throat.

"I still don't fully understand why you're here, but I'm grateful for the help." Henry plopped onto the front step. "It still drives me batshit crazy I can't fix these things myself anymore."

Ben understood that. How could he not? Sitting back onto his ankles, he placed the glass on the ground.

Henry stared at the porch. "After Holly's near fall, I knew something needed to give. I planned on coming up with a course of action this week."

"I guess it worked out that I was free today." Ben smiled. "I'm here to help and you seem to be enjoying bossing me around with the *right* way to do things." Ben chuckled, hoping to lighten the mood.

"Son." Henry looked at him. "There is a right way and a wrong way to do things. In this household, we always did things the right way. Even if that took more time." He puffed out his chest.

Ben's smile grew wider as he held up his glass. "I couldn't agree more."

They were both silent for a few moments while Henry leaned his back onto the handrail and watched as Ben worked to remove a rotted piece of wood. "Thank you, Ben."

"It's really no problem."

Looking away, Henry focused on a nearby tree. "I know I should start looking into a nursing home. That'd be the right thing to do. Especially now that Holly has you. I don't want her feeling obligated to be here all the time or help fix broken crap around the house."

Ben raised his brow. "Holly doesn't seem the one to fix items around the house without injuring herself."

"Oh, I didn't say she went about it unscathed, but she does do anything she can." Henry's eyes lit. "I think she's been saving some money to hire someone."

"I'm glad I came around, then. Neither of you will need to worry about fixing up this place or hiring some whack job to do it. Once we get the porch done we'll make a list of all the things you'd like to fix up and improve around the house. We'll tackle everything one step at a time. And, with you overseeing everything, this place will be good as new."

Henry scrutinized him. "Why are you so eager to help me fix up a house that's seen better days?"

He knew this was coming, it was only a matter of time. "I like you, Henry, and I know if the roles were reversed, you'd do the same for me."

"Are you sure that's your only reason for helping?" Henry asked.

"I am." He didn't mention he wanted any obstacle in Holly's way eliminated. He knew the old man tried to do right by his daughter, but with his predicament the house wasn't as safe as it could be for one accident prone walking disaster.

His mind quickly took a path it'd recently grown accustomed to. What if Holly had been pregnant when she fell out of the door? His whole body shuddered.

When she did get pregnant, he was wrapping her in bubble wrap from head to toe.

"You're right," Henry admitted. "If the tables were turned, I'd help out a decrepit old man get his house back in order."

"I wouldn't say decrepit," Ben laughed.

"But you would say old."

"You said it, not me."

Henry chuckled. "Does Holly know you're here?"

Ben sat back on his ankles once again. "Actually, she doesn't."

"Are you keeping it from her?" Henry's brow rose in question. Ben had to bite back his laugh. No one could ever question Henry's love for his daughter. He'd go head to head with anyone in a heartbeat.

"No, sir, I'm not."

"What did I tell you about calling me, sir? It makes me feel old."

Ben's face lit, before smirking. "Sure thing, sir. Won't happen again, sir."

"What does my little girl even see in you?" Henry laughed along with Ben.

"Hopefully a long future."

Henry's face hardened. "You love her, don't you?"

Before Ben could answer him, the phone rang. "Oh hell," Henry mumbled. "Hold that thought. I'll be right back." Henry slowly righted himself before rushing into the house to get the phone.

Ripley, who'd been watching them, made her way over and plopped herself in front of Ben demanding scratches. "You know, young lady, I think you've been hanging around Lord Waffles too much. You never used to be so demanding." Ripley in response rolled onto her back giving Ben her belly. "Yes, your highness. I didn't know I had two divas on my hands now." He started ruffling her belly making her

120

kick her legs out. "I can't wait to blame Holly for your newly found bossiness."

Ripley quickly turned away from Ben, ignoring his comment while moving back to the area in the shade. "I'm only good for a few measly scratches before you retreat back to your spot?" Ben narrowed his eyes at her before he let out a laugh. "I'm blaming Waffles."

Holly threw her car into park once she made it to her father's house. She quickly removed her seatbelt and exited the vehicle ready to find her dad.

Once she looked toward the house, she came to a complete halt seeing Ben. He was on his hands and knees with a toolbox to his right.

She was momentarily taken aback by his appearance. She couldn't help but stare at him. He wore dark jeans, that clearly had seen better days. Even with most of his lower half blocked by his position on the porch, she could see the jeans were ripped and well-worn. He also had on a light blue tee-shirt, that stretched across his chest. It had dark patches where his sweat had seeped through. The sleeves on his arms were taut as his muscles threatened to rip through the material.

When he flexed his upper arm, her breath hitched.

Ben looked like someone she'd read about in a blue-collar romance novel that dripped with sexy men. The only thing he was missing was a utility belt around his waist.

"Pumpkin, aren't you supposed to still be at work?" Her dad's voice broke her trance.

She looked from her father back to Ben, who now stood and was giving her a grin that could melt ice.

Holly stared at her father ignoring Ben. "After your phone call, I knew I needed to get here right away." She moved toward the porch. "Why are you here, Ben?"

Ben's face brightened. "I wanted to help your dad around the house." He wiped his hands on his jeans.

For the first time in her life, Holly felt honest to God real heartbreak. Here in front of her stood the man that made her feel like she'd never felt before. His gaze held a passion she knew she'd never come close to seeing in another man's eyes again.

Knowing she was about to let go of that made her heart break that much more. She knew she had a choice. A choice to save her father from going to a nursing home and after the text message she'd received not long after she hung up with her dad, she knew she had no other option.

Closing her eyes, her heart shattered the impossible bit more as she recalled the message.

Just so we are clear. Unfortunately, I would hate for Ben's clients to find out he's lost his license. The Board of Veterinary Medicine has been so busy lately. I know how paperwork can easily be misplaced. I would hate for him to have to close up shop.

Looking at Ben, Holly realized she'd never jeopardize his career or happiness. No matter what her feelings were.

She looked between both men as he did her best to harden her heart. To her left, stood Ben. The man she felt completed her like no other would or could. To her right, stood her father. The man who raised her and was always there for her.

In her heart she knew her next actions would hurt them

both. She just hoped in time they'd grow to forgive her and she could forgive herself.

With any luck a day many years from now, when she so happened to run into Ben, probably with his wife and family by his side, the heartbreak would have faded. Even if only a little.

Holly took a deep breath preparing for her next words. "You need to leave, Ben."

At her unexpected words, Ben jumped up and quickly descended the stairs to stand in front of her. The worry on his face was almost too much for her to handle. "What's wrong, Holly?"

Make him hate you. Give him no other choice but to leave.

"The only thing that's wrong is you thinking you can come over to *my* father's house and shove the fact he can't fix anything in his face. Just because your dad's dead doesn't mean you can hone in on mine." She wanted to vomit.

"Excuse me?" Ben took a step back as if her words slapped him.

"Young lady," her father scolded.

"I mean it, Ben, get your shit and leave. You're not welcome here." Ben took another step back this time holding his gut like he'd been punched.

"Holly Flanagan, what has gotten into you?" Her dad started making his way down the porch steps.

Holly's eyes burned with unshed tears. *Put the nail in the coffin.* She tore her eyes from Ben and looked at her father. "Go inside, I'll be there in a second, and we can discuss the issues. But first, I need to make sure Ben takes his mutt of a dog and leaves."

"Holly!"

"Get inside now, Dad!"

Henry looked from his daughter to Ben. Her gut clenched when he looked as though he'd still been sucker punched.

Holly's world was falling apart. Everything she felt inside of her, broke. Now he'd hate her and although that's exactly what she wanted from him, seeing the pain in his eyes would haunt her for the rest of her life.

"I'm only going inside because this is not how you normally act, Holly. I'm disappointed in you. I'm gonna let you two talk but listen here, little girl. I'm not sure about the honing in on your father part, but the only one who shoved my disability and inadequacy in my face, is *you*." He turned on his heel and stormed inside.

Holly closed her eyes as the hurt washed over her. Hearing she's now a disappointment to her father broke her beyond repair.

This is why you don't fall in love. It only leads to heartbreak and destruction for all.

"Holly?" Ben whispered.

She couldn't open her eyes. She knew if she did, the pain in Ben's eyes would take the last bit of control she held.

The tears fell down her cheeks with no stop in sight.

Ben placed his hand under her chin forcing her to look at him. "Open your eyes, baby."

She wouldn't.

She couldn't.

"I can fix whatever is going on," he pleaded with her. "Let me fix it. Please, Holly."

How could he still want to help her? How could he still be standing here trying to fix *her*?

Holly's control snapped. Her eyes shot open as her fists pounded into his chest pushing him backwards. "You can't fix this. You can't fix any of this. It's all your fault to begin with. Before you I had a normal life. I never had to worry about anyone other than my dad and now you've come in here and screwed up everything! I wish I never went to that dumb dog park that day. I wish I never met you." The realness of the situation was too much for her. She crumbled to the ground, her body shaking with sobs.

Ben instantly followed, holding her in his arms while she openly sobbed. Her shoulders shook as she let the events of the morning finally took its toll on her.

Ben pulled her into his lap encasing her in his arms, as he used his body to shield her from the outside world. "It's okay, baby, I'm here. Everything is going to be okay." He rocked her gently.

Holly wanted to pull away. She wanted to stand strong, but as she tried to grab at the courage she found herself clinging to Ben's shirt, pulling him closer instead.

How could being in Ben's arms make her feel safe? And why was he still willing to hold her, especially after what she'd said?

Pushing those thoughts away she cried.

She cried for her father and pain she'd caused him.

She cried for Ben and all of the hurtful things she'd said.

She cried for the love she knew she'd lost.

She cried for all of the pain she put everyone through.

She cried for her one real chance of happiness being ripped away.

CHAPTER FIFTEEN

BEN ROCKED Holly in his arms as he tried to wrap his head around the last few minutes. From the shocked look on Henry's face, which he was sure mirrored his own, to the pain in Holly's eyes as she spoke.

He knew something was very wrong. Although her comments about his father stung, he knew every word out of her mouth was not really her.

Even as Holly's words echoed through his head, he knew he couldn't believe them.

He wouldn't.

Ripley sat beside them looking from Holly to him. Even she was at a loss for what to do. Squeezing Holly tighter Ben waited for her gut-wrenching sobs start to slowly subside.

Once he knew they were under a manageable control, he lifted her chin so he could look at her. "Talk to me, Holly, Please."

She shook her head as he saw more tears pool in her eyes.

"Please, Holly." He rested his forehead on hers. "Let me

know what's going on. I can't fix it unless you tell me what the problem is."

She pulled back from his embrace to stare at him. The sadness in her eyes felt like a knife right through his chest.

"I-I..." Her voice hitched. "Ben, I don't know what to do!"

He placed his hand behind her head and brought her onto his chest as another sob escaped her. "Shh, it's okay, baby, we can work through anything."

She kept her head on his chest as she spoke, "When my dad couldn't go back to work, I took on all his bills."

As she spoke, the pain and concern in her voice broke him.

"Then all of a sudden his medical bills started coming in. I realized I couldn't do it all no matter how hard I tried or how much money I brought in. Before I knew it the bills started falling behind. I never wanted to burden my dad about it, so I never told him how bad it really is. I planned on getting a second job so I could at least get his mortgage up-to-date. When I met you, I guess I got distracted and it slipped my mind. Then today when I was at work I received a wake-up call."

Ben rubbed her back. If it was a money issue, he'd gladly take care of whatever she needed. Even if that meant tapping into the money his father left him. "Baby, if you're worried about money I can help you."

She shook her head pulling away from him. "It's not about the money or you helping. Besides, I'd never allow you to help with that. It's everything else, including the behind payments."

Ignoring her brush off of his offered financial help, he gently spoke, "Okay, explain it to me, Holly. Explain what 'everything' is. What was this wake-up call? What happened?"

She looked away from him.

"Holly. Talk."

"I can't lose my job, okay! It's the only income I have to help my dad. He means the world to me, and if that means I have to let you go in the process than I have to. No matter how much it hurts me I have to take care of him."

Ben's eyebrows knitted together. "I don't understand." Why would being with him make her lose his job?

She looked toward the trees in the yard. Her shoulders slumped as she took a deep breath. "Your mother has more pull than I ever thought possible."

What the fuck? His mother had something to do with this? There was a small part of him that wasn't all that surprised, though. His mother would find anything that made him happy and would try and destroy it. Holly included.

Knowing his mother was behind Holly's distress had every muscle in his body tighten. He needed to know more. He was only a few seconds from snapping. "Explain," he demanded.

Holly's body tensed at his hard words at first but she then firmed her jaw and looked him in the eyes. The determination he admired about her was back. "She showed up at the library this morning and told me if I wanted to keep my job I had to stop seeing you."

"What?!" *This had to be a fucking joke.*

Holly sat in his lap a little straighter as she continued. "She tried to pay me knowing I'm so far behind on my dad's bills. This house..." She gestured behind him. "...is about to be foreclosed on. I've been trying to work out a payment plan with the medical companies, so I can rearrange more money to the mortgage, but no one wants to budge." Tears pooled in her eyes once more with defeat. "She thought she could give me money to fix my problems, but I'd have to stop seeing you. No one bosses me around, Ben. No one. When she offered me the money I told her to shove it. When I thought she finally got the picture, she casually mentioned she knows four of the five library board members and she'd have me fired in one phone call. I thought she might be bluffing, but I still panicked. Obviously, her threats have merit. Not five minutes later my dad called asking when I'm coming over next because the bank called him." Her whole body slumped. "She said I had a choice. Pick my father and I wouldn't lose my job or pick you and I lose everything." She pulled out her phone and shoved it in his face. "And, so will you."

Ben read the screen as he did his best to digest everything Holly had said. His anger toward his mother was at an all-time high. Once the words on her phone registered, he saw red. "That fucking bitch," he growled.

He took Holly's phone and swiped through the message. Sure enough, it came from his mother's business phone. The same phone that *used* to belong to his father. "I'll fucking end her."

"You can't!" Holly pleaded. "She'll destroy you. She has the means to do it. She made it clear she owns this town."

He quickly pulled Holly into his arms. "She can't do anything."

"She already has."

In his mind, his mother was as good as dead at this point. She'd crossed one too many lines this time. "Do you trust me?"

When he looked into her eyes, he saw her trust in him. With her quick nod, he kissed her forehead.

"Good. First, let's take care of this one step at a time. I want you to go inside with your dad and call the bank. Find out how much is owed on the house. Then round up his medical bills. I'll take care of it."

"No!" Holly yelled. "I would never let you do that."

She tried to pull out of his embrace, but he wouldn't allow it. "You're not *letting* me do anything."

"You don't get it, Ben. Even if I won enough money in some lottery and paid everything off, if we stay together *you* lose everything. If she can easily manipulate the board of directors for the library or even a bank official, she could definitely follow through on her threats. I can't do that to you. I can't be the cause of you losing everything you've worked so hard for."

The concern for him and his happiness, overwhelmed him. "Holly, I promise you she can't do anything to my career."

"Yes, she can." He heard the desperation in her voice, causing him to reach out and hold her chin. "No baby, she can't. Even if she went to the state's veterinarian board and demanded my license be removed, she'd get nowhere."

"How can you be so sure?"

He smiled at her. "Seeing as I'm personal friends with half of the members and one of my dad's oldest friends is on the board, I'm safe."

"What does that even mean?"

"I can say we're not the only ones that aren't fond of Barbra Richman. She wouldn't have a leg to stand on."

"Fine, so you know the board, that doesn't mean she can't file complaints, or like she said make paperwork disappear. If she can ruin me, a measly librarian, with no sweat if she put in a little effort she'd destroy you."

"Baby, don't you think if she had the power to revoke

my license, she would've already done it? She's been trying to force me to work at Richman Industries since my dad died."

Holly stared at him blankly.

"The woman that birthed me is a manipulative bitch. She stops at nothing to get what she wants. If she had any chance of taking away my license she would have done so already. She can't do anything to jeopardize my practice. I promise."

Holly's face fell. "I don't understand why she'd go through all this trouble."

"I wish I could tell you, Holly, I really wish I could." He kissed the top of her head. "Now, I want you to go inside and talk to your dad. Call the bank and get all his bills in order."

When she opened her mouth to object, he stopped her. "Now. Holly."

She crossed her arms over her chest, her stubbornness back in full force. "And what makes you think I'll listen to you?"

Ben raised his brow. "Go inside, Holly." He lifted her off his lap. "By the time I get back, I want to know everything that's owed."

She narrowed her eyes at him. "And where the hell do you think you're going?" she asked.

"I'm going to see my mother."

CHAPTER SIXTEEN

HOLLY MADE her way into the house. However, when she rounded the corner to the kitchen the look on her father's face stopped her dead in her tracks. The confusion and hurt in his eyes caused her stomach to bottom out.

"Are you going to explain to me what happened out there?" her father's harsh tone echoed through the room.

"I'm sorry." She resigned herself. What more could she say?

"You're sorry?" His right brow rose.

"It's been a terrible morning."

"That is no excuse, young lady." He stood from the kitchen table then made his way over to her. He pulled her into his arms. "Hearing those cries broke me in two, sweetheart. I never want to hear that pain come from you again."

Holly pulled herself deeper into her father's embrace. How did she end up so lucky to have both the men in her life care so deeply about her? Sure, her father might be disappointed in the situation, but he'd never turn his back on her. Instead, he pulled her closer rubbing a small circle on her back letting her know everything would be okay. "I'm sorry, Dad," she whispered.

Giving her shoulder a quick squeeze, he motioned to the table. "Come, sit. Let's go over what happened."

"Okay." Blindly, Holly reached down to her side and pat Ripley on the head who had followed her inside. She hoped the dog would give her strength. "I don't really know where to start other than this morning."

"That sounds like a good place."

Holly tried to smile, but the gesture fell flat. "First, we need to get some things out of the way."

Henry looked at her slightly confused. "Okay."

"I haven't been honest with you." She took a deep breath.

"What do you mean?" He cocked his head to the side, studying her.

"The bills haven't been as up-to-date as I would like."

Both of his brows shot to the ceiling, one slightly higher than the other.

"I've fallen behind on everything." Holly's head fell in defeat. "I know I should have done better. I've disappointed you as a daughter. I should have tried harder."

Henry pulled her into his arms as tight as he could. "Holly, Pumpkin. Don't say that. Why didn't you tell me things weren't going well?"

"I didn't want to burden you. You've taken care of me your whole life. It's my turn to take care of you."

"We're family, Holly. Family sticks together and when one of us is struggling, all of us are struggling." He kissed the top of her head.

Pulling back, she did her best to look at her father through her watery gaze. "I realize I should have told you and I'm sorry for keeping everything a secret." She placed her palm on the side of his face that drooped. "After seeing you struggle after the blood clot and how hard it was for you to give up something you loved, I couldn't put you through anything that would hurt you again. I couldn't see that look of devastation on your face one more time."

Henry watched her with the pain in his eyes burrowing into her. "So, you took on everything so your old man wouldn't feel sorry for himself?"

Doing her best to lighten the mood she shrugged, before saying, "Well, when you put it that way, it sounds silly."

Henry kissed her head. "It is silly, Pumpkin."

"I promise to be more honest with you."

"That's all I ask for. That's all any father asks for."

She pulled herself from her father's arms. "You might want to sit down, Dad."

He looked at her quizzically.

"If honesty is what you want, I'm going to tell you everything."

Her father moved to the kitchen table before sitting. "I'm ready."

Ben stormed into Richman Industries ready to murder.

The moment he made it through the lobby, the cold dread he felt anytime he entered the building started to seep in. He did his best to avoid this place. Nothing good ever came from being inside of here.

Making his way past the receptionist, he headed toward the elevator. Stepping inside, he hit the top floor. He knew the layout all too well. As a child, he spent countless days playing at the foot of his father's feet. This whole building had been his personal playground.

He used to love the days his father took him to work.

Now the thought of stepping one foot inside of Richman Industries made him sick to his stomach.

When he reached the top floor the elevator doors opened. With a determination he didn't know he had he headed toward his father's old office.

"Mr. Richman, it's so nice to see you again," his mother's assistant greeted.

Ben took a controlled breath. He wasn't angry with her assistant and he refused to take it out on her. "Is Barbra in her office?"

"Yes, your mother is in there." She beamed at him doing her best to stick out her chest and entice him, which caused him to roll his eyes.

"She's no mother of mine." He blazed past her and threw open the office door.

There in front of him sat his mother. She had absolutely no right to sit where he sat. She was a fucking fraud. Always had been, and always will be.

Hearing the door open, Barbra looked from what he assumed was a fashion magazine and eyed him. The smug smile that spread across her face sent new waves of anger to course through his body.

"Benjamin, it's so nice of you to have stopped by," she sneered while sitting back in the chair.

"Cut the crap, Barbra."

She should win an award for the fake look of hurt and confusion that swept across her face. "Whatever do you mean?"

Ben walked toward her. "You've got to be fucking kidding me, *mother*. I knew you were a slithering bitch, but I never thought you'd stoop so low."

His mother straightened, her fake act dropped. "Oh son,

135

haven't you figured it out by now? I will do *whatever* I need to in order to get what I want." She smirked at him.

Ben fisted his hands at his sides trying to control his rage. "You're a fucking piece of work. How dare you go to Holly and threaten her and her father? Do you really think you have this much pull? Newsflash, *Barbra*, you're nothing around here."

Her eyes hardened. "I'm everything in this town."

Ben took a step closer to his mother. "You're a fucking joke. No one can stand you. They only tolerate you because you're unfortunately the head of Richman Industries."

"Oh, Benjamin." Her hurt act made its appearance once again. "Don't you understand? I only want to help you. I'm doing this all *for* you. Your words hurt me." She had the gall to place her hand over her heart.

"You are not doing this for me. You've never done a damn thing for me in my life."

She sat back in her seat. "How could you say that? I'm your mother. The only mother you'll ever have."

"Not anymore." He turned, ready to start his plans to take her down once and for all.

Barbra's features darkened. "You've always been an ungrateful bastard. Now that you have that cow in your life you think you're better than the rest of us," she spat.

Ben spun around, his eyes narrowed as he glared at her. "What did you just say?"

"You heard me, you ungrateful nuisance. As a mother, I've done everything I could to help you succeed. You were supposed to take the head of Richman Industries when your father died. I've groomed you for this moment, but you know what you did instead? You took everything I've ever done for you and threw it in the trash. Not only that, you think spending each day with mangy flea infested creatures makes you better than everyone else. Your silly clinic ruined you."

"*You* ruined me."

"I did no such thing. I tried to help you. Even your father tried to help you."

Ben's blood boiled at the surface of his skin as his lips flattened. "Don't fucking bring him into this. He'd still be here if it weren't for you."

Barbra crossed her arms over her chest as she smirked at him. "You're so naïve."

"Fuck off."

"Seriously Benjamin, do you really think your father would approve of you mingling with disgusting creatures all day? Not to mention, you are now associating with that... can you even call her a *woman?*"

Ben's control snapped. He leaned over the desk entering her personal space. "Listen here, bitch. Get your story straight. Dad paid for my practice. He *never* wanted me to follow in his footsteps. He wanted me happy and so help me God, if you so much as look in the direction of Holly or her father again I will end you."

Barbra laughed. "Oh really, *son.* Do you really believe *you* of all people have enough pull in this town to do anything to me?"

For the first time since entering the room, Ben smiled. "Why yes, Barbra, I do."

She stared at him a few moments, trying to call his bluff. When she got nowhere she reached for the phone. "I guess you leave me no choice." She picked up the receiver. "I do hope your *plaything* has another job lined up. Oh wait..." She smiled at him. "I know she doesn't."

Ben snatched the phone out of her hands slamming it

onto the desk. "Fucking Christ. You're seriously messed up in the head."

"Is it messed up in the head to want what's good for you?"

He threw his hands up in disbelief. "In your eyes what's good for me is to destroy the woman I'm in love with?"

"You do not love that dreadful woman."

"Yes, I do love her. She makes me whole. I've never in my life wanted someone more than I want Holly." He placed his hands on her desk leaning even closer into her space. "And I will destroy anyone that thinks they can hurt her."

"Please, you can't do anything."

"Watch me."

"It sure is a shame, Benjamin. I wonder how her father will feel about losing his home." She opened the magazine on the desk and started thumbing through it dismissing him.

Ben saw red.

He might have lost his own father to his crazy mother's demanding ways, but he'd be damned if he lost Henry too. No one could ever replace his father, but when Henry came into his life, much like when Holly did, the void he'd felt for years slowly started to disappear.

God he hated her. He hated everything about her. It was time to bring out the big guns. The pieces of information he'd had in his possession for years that he let stew in case he ever needed them.

Ben's blood rushed with adrenaline. It was time. He knew his mother thrived on confrontation. If he wanted to end her, he knew the perfect way to do it.

Ben straightened before popping his left hip on the side of the desk. Casually, he pulled out his phone and started thumbing through it. "I didn't know you cared so much about me," he remarked, looking at her through his peripheral vision.

Barbra's posture switched to one of a champion. "Of course I care, Benjamin. You're my son."

"I see that now." He nodded.

"I'm so glad you're finally coming to your senses." Barbra excitedly opened the desk drawer taking out a calendar. "Now that you realize where you belong, I've got a list of events for you to attend." She looked at him. "You know, schmooze the investors so we can get to their checkbooks. I know quite a few of them have daughters your age, some a little younger."

He felt the bile rise in this throat.

"Oh, the Jackson's have hinted recently how they want to see their daughter married to someone who aligned with their views. Howard Jackson owns a textile company a few cities over." Barbra clasped her hands together. "Could you imagine the income we can acquire if we merged with them?"

Ben's gut clenched. "You mean, you'll sweep in for a hostile takeover?"

The evil gleamed in his mother's eyes. "Of course."

"And you think it would be best if I marry someone like the Jackson's daughter?"

"She'd be perfect on your arm. Everyone will be in complete envy of her and of you."

Ben continued to swipe through his phone looking at pictures he'd sneakily taken of Holly throughout their time together. "And envious of you, no doubt."

Barbra's smile widened. "Precisely."

He looked at her face. "I have a question for you, *mother?*"

She nodded.

"Have you ever heard of a person that goes by *Douglas?*"

Her eyebrows knitted together. "I cannot say that I have."

"Huh?" Ben put his phone back into his pocket. "Before Dad died, he let me in on a little secret."

Barbra's mouth thinned. "What secret is that?"

"Toward the end, Dad stopped trusting you. He had a feeling you were up to no good, but he couldn't quite put his finger on it."

"What are you saying, *Benjamin?*"

Ben looked her dead in the eyes. "Did you know private investigators can find out *anything?* Including insider trading, threats, transferring funds from the company to an offshore account in the Bahamas that just so happens to have a monthly transfer that matches the exact amount deposited into your separate account each month?"

Barbra paled.

"Interesting how those funds have somehow always avoided the tax man. Speaking of the tax man..." Ben tapped his finger on his chin. "I wonder what the going rate for tax evasion is right now?"

"You wouldn't. I'm your mother."

Ben lifted a brow as he smiled at her. "You've taught me so well over the years. I know I can ruin you in, how do you like to say it? Oh, yeah, one phone call."

Barbra's face hardened, her lips thinning. "I'll destroy you first."

"I dare you to try." He pulled out his phone.

"What do you want?"

This time when Ben looked at her, he saw nothing but pure hatred. This should have been the woman to protect him from the world. This should have been the woman that wanted him to be happy and follow his dreams. This should have been the woman who was beyond excited that he'd found the person he wanted to spend the rest of his life with. Instead, she was the woman that killed his father with her greedy ways. She stole from the company his father worked himself to the bone to make successful. And worst of all, this was the woman that threatened the happiness of Holly and her dad, who he'd now loved like his own father. "For you to fucking disappear. Give this company to the board and leave."

Her eyes narrowed.

"And listen clearly, Barbra, if you ever fucking threaten my family again I won't hesitate to make the call."

"I'm your only family," she sneered.

"You've never been my family."

She sat straighter in her chair. "You'll have no one."

"You're wrong." Ben chuckled. "Holly and her dad are the *only* family I need."

CHAPTER SEVENTEEN

After telling Henry everything, including Barbra and her threats, he wanted to explode. He demanded Holly drive him to Richman Industries so he could give her a piece of his mind. Holly couldn't blame him, she felt the same way.

After talking him down a little bit, she knew he needed time to digest everything. Especially the financial situation. He wasn't too happy about taking Ben's offered help, but at this point, neither one of them had much of a choice.

Once she gathered the documents Ben requested and gave her dad another kiss on the cheek, she contemplated on where to go.

Before the shitstorm of the morning, their original plan was to have dinner at Ben's house. He'd given her his extra key and told her to bring Waffles over after work.

Could she still follow through with those plans?

There was a part of her that wanted to abandon them and cocoon herself in her apartment. However, there was a bigger part of her that wanted to be surrounded by Ben's stuff.

When the hell did I get so weird and needy?

Shaking herself from the thoughts Holly knew after a day like today there was only one choice.

Ben.

Always Ben.

Not to mention she was sure whatever hell Ben encountered with his mother, he would need her as much as she needed him.

Not being able to help it, she worried her bottom lip. *What if Ben decides his mother is right? Or what if he decides this whole thing is too much work and gives up?*

Instantly, her heart tightened.

No, that wouldn't be the case. She trusted Ben. Relationships like this didn't happen every day, and Holly knew that. She had to let go of the fear.

Ripley barked from the back seat clearly agreeing with her.

"Are you a mind reader now?" Holly looked in the rearview mirror at the dog.

Ripley barked again.

"You're right, Rip. Let's go get your comrade." Shaking her head at Ripley jumping around the back seat, Holly turned onto her street ready to retrieve Waffles from her apartment and head *home.*

Sitting in Ben's living room, Holly's nerves started to get the better of her. At this point, she didn't *think* anything else could go wrong, but based on her track record she knew it could.

Ripley and Waffles were playing in the kitchen, hopefully not developing a master plan to jump on one of their backs, using the extra boost to reach the treats on the counter. She honestly wouldn't put it past them. Ever since bringing them together, they've done a bang-up job of hatching elaborate plans.

She smiled to herself thankful for the distraction.

From the corner of her eye she saw Twitch make his way out of the other room. She couldn't help but smile at the kitten. Ben brought him to his house on Friday.

When Holly had asked why he didn't bring him to her apartment, his excuse consisted of, "I'm the trained professional, and I want Twitch to be close by just in case something happens."

What a complete load of crap that was.

Other than the twitch he still had, the kitten was in perfect health.

Holly knew the reason Ben wanted Twitch at his place. He wanted a reason for them to end up at his house rather than her tiny apartment. She was sure it had something to do with his king-size bed versus her full.

Chuckling to herself, Holly couldn't entirely blame him. Two people, two dogs, and now a cat...

"Hey, Twitchy," Holly cooed as the groggy kitty who'd apparently been sleeping, made his way further into the room. Once Twitch heard her voice, his ears perked. He ran toward Holly jumping onto the couch to be next to her.

Maybe there will be an animal in this house that will listen to me.

Twitch settled in next to her, his little twitch knocking into her every now and then. Even though most people would consider it an unwanted side effect, it made her heart melt and only made her love him more.

Holly scratched behind his ear, enjoying the purr that erupted from him.

That's when she heard the front door open.

Holly braced herself as she waited for whatever form of Ben was going to come through the door.

Ripley and Waffles came flying into the living room as soon as the door opening registered in their little minds.

Typical. Neither one of them cared she was dying on the couch just a measly few feet from them. They only wanted Ben.

As Ben entered the room he smiled at her before dropping to his knees to greet the pups. "Hey guys," he cooed. He did his best to keep himself upright from the onslaught of kisses.

Holly watched as he scratched both dogs who simultaneously plopped onto their backs demanding belly rubs. Knowing once the ceremonial greeting of the dogs was over, he'd look at her. She bit her bottom lip knowing that moment would come any second.

"What havoc did you two cause while I was away?" he asked.

Ripley replied in a deep bark followed by Waffles whining when Ben pulled this hand away.

"Sounds wonderful," Ben laughed before righting himself. When he finally looked at Holly the smile on his face made her stomach bottom out.

What does a smile mean?

Throwing his key on the nearby coffee table, Ben made his way to her. "I see Twitch is right at home in your arms."

Holly looked at the sleepy cat who'd made himself quite comfortable on his back.

As she looked at the sleeping baby, Holly's vision blurred with tears. She didn't know when her life had gotten so intertwined with Ben's, but she knew this conversation could go one of two ways. He'd either tell her he took care of his mother and her job and father were safe or he'd changed his mind.

Wait a second.

What if he murdered her and he now needed me to help him hide the body? Holly couldn't be an accessory to murder. Sure, she loved the guy but she had a demanding dog and now a kitty to take care of. Not to mention, her father. Plus, she would never look good in a jumpsuit. No one ever did.

Feeling her emotions about to snap she shot her head to Ben. "What happened? Tell me."

"Tell you what?" he asked, smugly.

"Jerk."

"Oh." He leaned over her lap kissing her forehead before standing. "Are you referring to what happened when I saw my mother?"

She narrowed her eyes. Never mind her being the accessory to murder, she was about to be the person committing the crime. "Don't make me throw something at you."

"All you have in your lap right now is Twitch and I know you'd never throw him."

Well damn, he had her figured out. "You're right, I'd never throw him but I will take off my shoe and aim right for your head."

"So violent." He cocked his brow.

Holly's left eye twitched.

"Have you ever realized when you're annoyed your eye starts to twitch?" He pat the kitten behind the ear, waking him. "I guess you two are perfect for each other with the twitching and all."

Ben reached around the cat plucking him from her lap. After giving him a chaste kiss on his head, he placed Twitch on the other end of the couch where he promptly fell right back asleep.

All of a sudden, Holly was yanked off the couch and into Ben's arms. Not giving her any time to protest, he kissed her like a starving man.

After a few seconds she remembered she needed answers and him playing around was going to get him in an early grave. Placing her palms on his chest, she pushed him away. "Ben, so help me God I will hurt you. What the hell happened with Barbra? Do I need to find a new job? Oh crap, that's it right?" She started pacing. "I need to find a new job. One that will pay enough for my bills *plus* my dad's." She snapped her head to Ben. "Do you think the bank will still foreclose on the house if I plead with them?" She didn't let him answer as she continued her pacing. Unfortunately, in her hasty movements, she misjudged the coffee table's edge and smacked her shin.

Before she knew it, she started toppling over headed directly for the floor. She held out her hands ready for impact. However, like every other time Ben was around during one of her mishaps, she found herself in his arms rather than on the floor.

"Jesus, Grace." He laughed, pulling her into his arms. "I might need to wrap you in bubble wrap now, not just when you're pregnant."

Holly jumped out of his arms. "What?"

Ignoring her question Ben leaned forward kissing the tip of her nose. He then moved to the couch and plopped down next to Twitch.

Holly's eyes started to twitch again. *He wants me to kill him, doesn't he?*

Taking a deep breath, she decided to face one obstacle at a time. But, mark her words the whole pregnant talk will be discussed later. Bubble wrap, who did he think he was? "Ben, if you don't tell me what the hell happened between you and your mother so help me God, I will take Ripley, Waffles, and Twitch and leave." She glared at him. "And you *won't* be able to follow us."

Ben's eyes danced as his right brow quirked. "You gonna steal my dog?"

"She likes me better." She pointed to the dogs. Waffles now used Ripley as his own personal pillow. "Plus, I can't break up the dynamic duo."

"And, what makes you think I wouldn't be able to follow you?" He crossed his arms over his chest.

"You can't follow me when you're rolling around on the floor searching for your balls after I kick them so hard they find a new home deep inside your other organs."

Ben cupped between his legs making Holly raise her chin in triumph.

After a few minutes, she placed her hands on her hips, waiting for Ben to stop his dramatics. Once she realized he wasn't going to stop, her eyes narrowed. "Talk," she growled.

"Oh, I like it when you get all dominant." He laughed before pulling her onto his lap. Within seconds he had her positioned with both of her legs on either side of his.

"No, Grace..." He gave her a chaste kiss on the lips. "You do not need to find yourself a new job. You do not need to worry about your father or his finances. No, you are not taking our babies and leaving town. You are staying right here, beside me, forever. Got it?"

Holly's brows shot to the ceiling. Was he seriously going to play with her? Okay, great, she didn't need to worry about her job or father, but she needed to know what happened between him and Barbra. *Was she dead?*

"Freakin' tell me what happened, Ben, or I will pinch you!"

Ben's belly laugh echoed throughout the room as he kissed her forehead. "Now I can't have the dreaded pinch pirate come after me, can I?"

When Holly made the move to pinch him, he held out his hands in surrender. "Okay, jeez I went to Richman Industries and explained to Barbra if she ever threatened someone I love again she'd lose everything."

Someone I love... Holly froze. *He loves me?*

"My father was a smart man, Grace. He knew something wasn't right. He might have loved her at one point, but somewhere along the line he realized something wasn't quite as innocent as he wanted to believe when it came to Barbra Richman."

Pain flashed in Ben's eyes as he talked about his dad.

"All of the information his private investigator found on her was handed to me after his death. I never planned on using it against her. She's still my mother and as much as I despised her for her role in my father's death, she was the woman that gave me life."

"What?" Her mouth fell open.

"I know this doesn't make sense. Hell, it doesn't make sense to me. I should've outed her right after my dad died. But I didn't. Maybe there was a part of me that still looked at her as family. I don't really know." He rubbed Holly's arm in slow circles. "After what you said this morning and what she did, I had a choice. Do you want to know what choice I had?"

Holly nodded, biting her bottom lip.

"Given a choice between her and you, I will always choose you. I knew what I had to do, baby." Ben placed his hand on her chin making Holly face him.

He looked deeply into her eyes. The passion in his gaze made her breath hitch.

"I love you, Holly Flanagan."

"You love me?"

"Yes baby, I love you. I love everything about you. From your sense of humor to your mouth watering body and the way you stumble through life tripping and falling into everything." The corner of his mouth turned up as love poured out of him.

"Hey!"

"I don't call you Grace for nothing."

Holly looked into Ben's eyes and saw the love he had for her. Everything melted away from them. It was just them, two people that loved each other. A few hours ago she thought she'd lost everything: her father, her job, and the love of her life. But here in front of her, Ben wanted to give her all of those and more back. He wanted to give her what she'd always craved and never thought she'd be lucky enough to feel.

Holly captured her lips with his, as she poured all her emotions into their embrace. She loved him. She loved him more anything in this world.

When she pulled away, Holly rested her head on his forehead. "You came into my life and it felt like I was thrown onto a roller coaster. It's been nonstop since the day at the park. Somewhere along the way, though, you made me fall in love with you, Ben. I don't know how, and I don't know why, but I love you."

Ben smiled a sexy crooked smile at her. "It was Lord Waffles. We've been in cahoots this whole time trying to get you to love me."

"Really? Is that so?"

"Yep. We developed this master plan the day at the

park. We knew all we needed to do was get you to stand in the right spot at the right moment and you'd be so enamored with my charm you couldn't help but fall in love with me."

"That's what happened?"

"One hundred percent." Ben kissed her lips. "That's my story and I'm sticking to it."

Holly chuckled as she shook her head. "What am I going to do with you?"

"Love me."

CHAPTER EIGHTEEN

BEN CUPPED Holly's cheeks in his hands as he pulled her into a kiss. Both their emotions were raw from the events of the morning, but as long as Holly was in his arms, he knew everything would be okay.

Hell, it would be better than okay.

He had Holly.

Ben nipped at her bottom lip causing a groan to escape from her.

Holly moved her hips, grinding against his lower half igniting every one of his nerve endings on fire. He growled as his dick threatened to break through his jeans.

The moment Ben felt the heat from her core, his eyes rolled back in his head. *God damn, she was perfect.* Ben placed his hands on her hips helping her grind against him.

Fuck he loved this woman.

Love.

He did love her. Ben loved everything about her. From her stubborn sass all the way to her diva dog. When Holly came into his life, he finally felt what he'd been missing all along.

Holly was the woman he planned on spending the rest of his life with.

And he couldn't wait.

As Holly continued to grind her hips against this dick trying to get more friction a hiss escaped him. She knew exactly what she wanted and would do whatever it took to get it.

Ben's thoughts were cut off the moment Holly reached between them to cup his dick through the material. A deep growl escaped him as he arched into her, giving her everything she wanted.

When he looked at her, he almost lost it. Her cheeks were red, her eyes clouded with passion.

Fuck she was perfect.

As her body rocked against him, he could feel the love that poured out of her.

Ben's body pushed against hers as the tension in the room thickened. He moved closer, kissing her neck before lightly nipping at her skin.

He needed more. He needed to taste her.

In one quick movement, he removed her hand from his dick and flipped them. He secured both of her wrists in his left hand above her head. Returning his head to the crook of her neck he inhaled deeply. "How the fuck do you always smell so good?"

"I shower daily," Holly remarked which made Ben laugh before shaking his head. *Only, Grace.*

He licked her neck once more. "It makes me want to taste every inch of you." He felt her pulse along his lips as he sucked gently on her skin.

"More," she begged, moving her neck to the side giving him better access.

Oh, he was going to give her more. He was sure of it.

Ben repositioned himself so he was cradled snuggly between her legs. Grinding against her center, she moaned.

Music to my ears.

That sound was something he planned on hearing many more times tonight.

Letting go of her wrists, Holly straightened as Ben reached behind him and pulled his shirt from his body. Tossing it to the side he reached for Holly's top and ripped it from her body causing a tearing sound to echo through the room.

"I'll kill you!"

"No, you won't." He laughed at the annoyed face Holly shot his way. Ignoring her, he cupped both of her breasts in his hands. Her hardened nipples peaked through the lace material of her bra. Flicking his thumbs over them, her body arched toward his touch, which only encouraged him more.

How did he end up this lucky to have someone so damn responsive?

A huge smile spread across his face. God, he loved this woman.

In his same skilled movement, he'd done with her shirt, Ben took the two cups of Holly's bra and ripped them apart. The lace gave way in seconds.

"Bras cost a million dollars!" She punched his chest.

He was going to have to invest stock in woman's lingerie, because he planned on ripping every scrap of underwear from her body for the rest of their lives. "I'll buy you another one."

"Hell no!" She glared at him. "You'd probably come out of the store with the most unsupportive scrap of nothing." She held up her breasts and his mouth watered. She looked like a goddess, offering her succulent desserts at his altar. "These big girls need support. I won't have you buying me garbage that makes these babies dangle down to my knees."

Diving his head between her chest he ignored every word out of her mouth as he took what she offered and worshiped them. Plus, as soon as he hit up the store he would buy exactly that. Less material meant less barrier.

Ben pulled her nipple into his mouth causing her to let out another moan. He sucked and tongued her peak as he used his other hand to tweak its twin.

Releasing her with a wet pop, he started working himself down her body kissing every inch of her as he went. When he reached her belly button, he dipped his tongue in while locking eyes with her.

The passion that stared back at him had his heart skip.

He kissed right below her belly button before he straightened himself. Quickly he removed her belt and with a few skilled movements, he had her naked beneath him.

"Why am I always the one that's naked while you've got most of your clothes on? This never makes any sense to me."

"I'm not as nice to look at as you are."

"The heck you say." Her brow quirked.

"It's true." Ben brought his head to her center. "I fucking love looking at you. You're perfect." Kissing the top of her mound, he looked at her. Holly's lower lip drew between her teeth.

"Yeah, but you're just as gorgeous to look at."

"Not to me." He kissed her mound again this time letting his tongue slip out. When he swirled it around her sensitive skin, she moaned, nearly making him snap.

Ben grabbed onto her hips pushing her back further to the arm of the sofa almost making her sit up straight. Placing one of his legs on the floor, he spread Holly's legs.

Taking a moment to lean back he gazed at her wanting

to burn this image into his mind forever. Holly spread wide for him, her legs bent and her chest rising and falling as she stared at him with nothing but love in her eyes.

His eyes moved back other core, the wetness he saw drove him to the brink. He had one goal right now, and that was making Holly come as many times as he could before the sun came up.

Slowly, Ben trailed his fringe across her stomach down to her center. He gently spread her lower lips as be brought his mouth to her ready to finally feast on the woman he loved.

As Ben's expertly skilled tongue worked her core, Holly thought she'd somehow died and gone to heaven. She pulled Ben's hair as he used his fingers to seek out her spot.

Whoa!

Holly could get used to this.

When Ben lightly grazed her clit with his teeth, her orgasm overtook her. Ben held her down as her hips tried to rocket off the couch.

"Holy shit," she panted as she felt every muscle in her body explode. After her body released, she opened her eyes to see Ben's smug face staring back at her.

She couldn't help the smile that spread across her own face. Yep, she could one hundred percent get used to this.

"You're breathtaking when you come." Ben kissed the inside of her thigh.

"Not as breathtaking as your dick." In one quick movement, Holly pushed Ben onto his back.

"Shit!" He stopped Holly's assault before he sat upward looking behind him.

Oh, no did she hurt him?

Ben reached behind him grabbing Twitch.

"Is Twitch okay?" How could she have forgotten? Poor kitten, he'd already been through so much, now he had to deal with almost being mushed to death by his parents.

The kitten looked at her and Ben with disgrace and demanded to be placed on the floor. Once he was on solid ground, he took off running but not before looking back at them one more time in shame.

Okay cool, now her kitten thinks she's some sex starved woman, and judge the crap out of her. At least he was okay.

"Did you see the look on his face?" Ben barked out a laugh.

"He's gonna hold this over us. I can feel it now." Holly smiled at Ben shrugging.

"Never a dull moment, is there?"

"Never." Holly stood holding out her hand for Ben to take it. With confidence in her stride, Holly led him to the bedroom. As she walked through the hallway, she couldn't help the feeling that spread through her. Before Ben she would have never dared to be openly naked in front of a man. Especially, a man that looked like Ben.

Glancing over her shoulder, she saw him blindly following her as he refused to take his eyes off her ass. Seeing where his attention was, Holly did the only thing she could do. She gave her ass a little shake. She wasn't instantly rewarded when a deep growl came from behind her.

The way Ben worshipped and loved her body sent another wave of confidence through Holly. If she'd known a sex god was all it took to skyrocket her self-esteem, she would have signed up for one years ago.

Holly shook her ass once more, causing a deeper noise to escape from Ben.

God, she loved him. With everything inside of her, she loved this man.

Once they made it to the bedroom, Ben pulled on her hand making her swing back toward him. He effortlessly caught her in his arms. Ben grabbed her hips lifting her into the air making Holly wrap her legs around his waist.

Don't mind if I do.

He pushed himself into her center. "Fuck, I can feel how hot you are through my jeans."

"Imagine how hot I'd feel if you took them off."

Tossing her onto the bed, Ben quickly removed his clothes. Within seconds he was on top of her, kissing his way up her body.

When he reached her face, he cupped her cheeks in his hands. "I love you, Holly."

"I love you too, Ben." And, she really did. She couldn't see herself without him in her life.

With one thrust, Ben pushed himself inside of her causing Holly's eyes to roll to the back of her head as she felt every movement. She was so full, she'd never get used to this feeling.

Ben's movements increased as he reached between them and sought out her clit. When he found it, he pinched. The electricity flowing through her body was enough to throw her over the edge one more time. "Oh man, oh man. I'm—"

Ben brought his lips to hers, cutting her off. He pushed his tongue past her lips seeking out her taste. He kissed her with such passion, she thought she would drown in it.

Tearing his mouth from hers Ben rested his head in the

crook of her neck as his movements became more erratic. "I can't hold on."

"Don't." She could feel herself teetering on the edge once again.

Ben moved harder and deeper as her body reached its peak. With one last pinch to her clit, the stars behind her eyes erupted.

"Fuck!" Ben's face contorted as she felt him empty himself deep inside of her.

He then collapsed on top of her, his breathing heavy. "Holy shit, Holly. You're gonna kill me one of these days." He wrapped his right arm around her waist as he laid his head on her chest.

"Right back at cha."

Her world sure as hell had become a whirlwind since Ben ran into her life. There was no doubt of that. But as she laid there with Ben she never wanted this to end.

Holly's smile widened as she realized Ben started tracing idle circles on her stomach. A stomach she desperately tried to hide so many times in the past. But with Ben, she finally felt free enough to not be ashamed.

This was her, take it or leave it, and if you didn't like her or her size you could see yourself out.

Why? Because, she had Ben and that's all she would ever need.

As Ben placed his hand on her stomach she couldn't help but imagine him doing the same thing as their baby grew inside of her.

Wait a second!

A baby? Their baby. She didn't know whether to laugh or cry. She never thought about having kids before, but now... She closed her eyes as she thought about it.

Hold on...

He'd wrap me in bubble wrap?

Holly smacked Ben's hand off her belly.

"Why'd you do that?" he asked, annoyed.

"You will *not* wrap me in bubble wrap."

Ben's brow rose as the challenge swam in his features. "Wanna bet?"

"Yeah, I wanna bet." She tried pushing him off her body to no avail.

"Oh, Grace, how I love your feistiness." His smug look made her eye twitch.

"My feistiness is gonna punch you in the teeth."

"Nope," he announced so sure of himself. "Your feistiness gets me hard." He pounced on top of her going between her legs.

How was he hard again so soon? Holly didn't have time to ask since he pushed himself inside of her. Their talk of babies and bubble wrap was going to have to wait until another time.

CHAPTER NINETEEN

Ben woke with Holly nestled on his chest. Ripley and Twitch slept at the foot of the bed, Lord Waffles was on his back with his legs in the air. He had wedged his way between Ben's legs, snoring.

He huffed out a chuckle at the crazy dog.

Ben couldn't help the feeling of warmth that rushed through him. He wanted every morning to be exactly like this.

Removing his eyes from the occupants of the bed, he looked around his room. Before he met Holly, he thought his house was enough. His bedroom used to be his sanctuary, but now, he realized it felt barren and cold.

His eyes focused on the dresser where Holly's overnight bag sat.

Glancing around his room again, he had the urge to go to her bag and remove her belongings and place them around his room.

The thought made adrenaline rush through his body, as his heart rate sped.

That's exactly what he needed in his house. He needed

Holly, and her belongings here on a permanent basis. She would make his house a home.

"What's got your heart racing?" Holly's groggy voice sounded from his chest.

"Morning, sleepy head." Ben kissed the top of her head.

"If your heart is racing 'cause you've got a stiffy, I'm gonna need to take a rain check. You wore me out last night."

Ben barked out a laugh as he placed his hand under her chin, pulling it upwards so he could kiss her lips.

"Eww morning breath." Holly pulled away.

"Are you saying I have morning breath?" He lifted his brow.

"No. I'm saying *I* probably have morning breath and I do not want to subject you to it. That shit is not all roses like they say in the movies or books."

"Noted." Deciding to ignore her, though, he pulled her into a deep kiss. When he pulled away from her lips, he winked. "That's what I think about your morning breath prejudice."

Rolling her eyes, she settled back into Ben's side. "This is nice."

He couldn't have agreed more. He kissed the top of her head once again. "Waffles sure thinks so." The dog's tongue hung out of his mouth as he snored away.

"That's my boy." Holly smiled. "Tongue out for days."

"That so?" Ben's eyes lit with mischief causing Holly to punch him lightly on the chest.

"You've got a one-track mind, mister."

"With you. *Always*."

She laughed, nodding her head. "Me too."

"Do you have work today?" he asked, looking at his

alarm clock. He didn't have to be at the clinic until nine forty-five, and right now, the clock only read six-fifteen.

"Yes, I work the morning shift from eight-thirty until three." She started scooting away from him. "That reminds me, I'm gonna need to get a move on if I plan on walking Waffles, having a shower, and actually eating breakfast before I head to work."

"I have a backyard, Grace," Ben announced. "I'll let Waffles out, and you can hop in the shower while I make us some breakfast."

"Don't call me Grace." She gave him a dirty look. "That all sounds fine and dandy, but I have to head to my apartment first. I forgot to grab work clothes with all of the stress of everything that happened yesterday."

Ben didn't like her response. Holly deserved every free moment she got. She shouldn't have to worry about heading home to get clothes to be at work on time.

He tilted his head to the side as he started to ponder her situation. The library was closer to her apartment and she did walk to and from work most days. But... fuck it. "Move in with me."

"Excuse me?" She tripped, falling over as she got out of bed.

"You heard me, Holly. Move in with me." He gestured with his hand around the room. "Look how empty everything is."

She glared at him as her lips diminished into a thin line. "You want me to move in with you so your house doesn't look as sad?"

"No, I mean yes," he backpedaled. "No...damnit."

"Go shopping and buy knickknacks to fill the space."

"That's not what I want." He swiped his hand over his face. *Use your adult words, Ben. Don't fuck this up.* Taking a deep breath, he started again, "I want *your* items in the empty spaces. I want to wake up every morning the same way I did today. I want Waffles pushing me out of bed every night demanding himself more room." Ben looked into her eyes. "I want you."

"So, it's not just my stuff you want?" Holly cocked her head to the side.

The corner of Ben's eyes crinkled as he smirked. "Why are you so stubborn?"

"Most people don't ask someone to move in with them by saying they need more stuff to fill the empty spaces."

He laughed at her upturned nose. "You have a point."

"I have a good point."

"What's your answer?"

Holly bit her bottom lip as she shrugged. "I don't know, Ben. Don't you think this is all going a little too fast? One moment you're hitting me in the face with a Frisbee and the next you're asking me to move in with you."

Ben rolled his eyes. "I am not even going to dignify that with a response." His words must not have registered because she continued, "And, what do you expect I do about work? I walk there every day. It's the only exercise I get."

Ben lifted his brow. "I'm pretty sure our horizontal tango counts as exercise."

"It does not!"

"It's pretty physical."

"You're such a man."

"And you love it." He pulled the sheets from his body causing Waffles to growl at being covered.

Ignoring the dog, he reached for his hardening dick, palming it. He winked. "You love it all."

Holly barked out a deep laugh before crawling onto the

164

bed. "I don't know if it makes me crazy or not, but I have some strange voice in the back of my head telling me to say yes."

"Listen to it," he said, reaching for her.

"What do I get out of it?"

"Other than this?" He held the base of his hard on.

"You're impossible."

Letting go of himself he maneuvered on the bed to be right next to her. "Say yes. You know you want to. Your apartment is tiny, and here we have a backyard for the dogs to play in. Twitch is already accustomed to his new home and well... I want you here. *All the time.*"

Holly sat on her knees before tapping her finger on her chin. "I don't know."

"Grace," he warned, which caused her to glare at him again.

"I'll never move in with a bossy pants."

"Holly Flanagan, do not make me bend you over and spank your ass," he said sharply.

Quick as lightning Holly moved in to give him a quick kiss before pulling away. "Fine. I'll move in."

After hearing the words and registering her trying to get away he pounced. He grabbed onto her waist flipping her under him. Straddling her legs, he started to kiss his way down her body. It was time to celebrate.

Holly sat at her desk with a huge smile on her face. After she agreed to move in with Ben, he'd thrown her onto her back and made her explode more times than she could count. She hoped living with him would mean many repeat performances exactly like this morning.

Wow, I am really going to do it. I'm going to move in with Ben. Her mouth formed into a lopsided grin. *Holy Crapolie.*

"That is a look of a very satisfied woman," Mildred announced, coming from around the corner, which made Holly smirk.

"I'm not all that surprised, though."

"What makes you say that?" Holly asked.

"Do you really think that hunk of man meat would let you go? I knew once you told him about what happened he'd figure out what to do." She pointed to Holly's face. "He obviously did."

Holly nodded.

"Here you are sitting at the job you'd thought you'd lose, after that wretched woman yesterday. I'd say Ben took care of everything."

"She was a bitch, wasn't she?" Holly agreed.

"That she was. I may or may not have looked up how to place a Voodoo curse on her after you ran out of here."

Holly shook her head. "Only you, Mildred."

"Of course, only me. Who else is going to take care of my chickadee?"

"I'm your chickadee?" Holly asked.

"You're like the daughter I never had."

Holly's heart warmed. "That's sweet, Mildred. I didn't think you did sweet, more feisty and nosy." She smirked. "But, I can honestly say, you've been like a mother figure to me too."

"Are you sure you don't mean to say sister? Can't you throw this old lady a bone and make me sound younger."

Holly laughed. "Sure."

"That's what I like to hear."

"Glad I can be of service to you."

"That's why I keep you around. Now, let me guess what put that smile on your face."

Holly shook her head with a laugh. "Have at it."

"After you bolted out of here like a bat out of hell, you smartly took my advice and ran right into your man's arms, spilled your guts and then he informed you he'd take care of it and then nailed you on the closest wall."

"Does your husband know you talk like this?"

"Where do you think I got it from?"

"Mildred," she said as her eyes gleamed. "I can truthfully say you're wrong. I didn't run into Ben's arms. I went to my dad's and Ben just so happened to be there. Get this? He was fixing the porch. Anyway, after a few crappy words on my part, he did say he would take care of it. He went right to his mother and gave her an ultimatum, but I must say you are correct on one part. Once he came home, he did nail me. More than once."

"Get it girl!" Mildred threw her fist in the air.

"And once again after he asked me to move in with him this morning."

"You better have said yes, missy. So help me God, if you didn't, I might be old but I *will* kick your butt from here all the way to Timbuktu."

Holly roared with laughter. "I said yes, you crazy old lady."

Mildred placed her hand over her heart. "Oh, thank God. I really didn't want to have to hurt you."

"There you are!"

Holly and Mildred snapped their heads to the front door.

Holly's stomach bottomed out when one angry Barbra Richman started charging right toward them.

CHAPTER TWENTY

ALL THE COLOR left Holly's face as her heart raced and her palms began to sweat. Quickly she glanced around the lobby as she tried to make sense of the situation. Why in the hell was Barbra here?

The Universe strikes again!

Swallowing hard, Holly pulled her eyes back to Barbra. The look that stared back at her held nothing but pure hatred.

Holly gulped as Barbra stormed toward them, her movements fast and precise.

Before Barbra made it to them, though, Mildred took a step forward. "What do we owe the pleasure of seeing the devil so early?" Mildred remarked. "I didn't think you came out during the day." She tapped her chin looking to the side. "Oh wait, that's vampires."

"This doesn't concern you, old woman," Barbra sneered which caused Mildred's eyebrow to skyrocket.

"The heck you say." Mildred shook her head. "What if you really are a vampire? I mean it would make sense you seem to have a fondness for sucking the life out of people. I understand the vampire realm is on a need to know basis kind of thing, but if you really are a blood-sucking creature, I want to know." She took out her pen and paper.

Barbra spun to face her. "Keep talking, you old crone and watch what I can do to you."

Mildred crossed her arms over her chest, daring Barbra to do anything. "Sounds like a vampire to me."

Although Mildred always found a way to make any situation entertaining, Holly knew it was better to cut this off at the pass. Plus, Holly was absolutely done with Barbra and her antics. Time to finally put this psycho in her place. Holly stood with her hands on her hips, jutting her chin toward her target. "You can't *do* anything, Barbra. You and I both know you can't do shit. Why are you even here? After what Ben told you I thought you'd be long gone by now." She shrugged. "Guess your freedom doesn't mean much to you."

Barbra's glare turned to Holly as her nostrils flared and her lips thinned. "This is all your fault. If it weren't for you and your meddling in my son's life he wouldn't have questioned me. It's because of *you* everything is falling apart."

"I wasn't the one that stole from the company." Holly marched closer pointing her finger at Barbra's chest. "You did all of this by yourself. Everything is falling apart because *you're* a piece of shit human being. You can't blame your actions on me." Holly turned away moving back toward Mildred.

"Keep your voice down, little girl," Barbra sneered toward Holly.

"Have you met me?" Holly pointed at herself. "I don't keep my voice down. It's not in my DNA."

"Just like having any sort of class isn't in your DNA."

"Get off your high horse, Barbs. Your insanity is showing." Holly rolled her eyes at the woman.

"Can you not handle the truth?" Barbra smiled, as she straightened.

Holly's brow shot to the ceiling. The smug look on Barbra's face made her skin crawl. Why in the hell would Barbra act proper all of a sudden? This woman really did have a few loose screws.

Shaking her head, Holly stated, "You're seriously not making any sense, you crazy halfwit."

Barbra chuckled before placing her hand on her upper chest, smiling.

Holly's eyes went round as she instinctively took a step back. Clearly, Ben's mother had snapped. If the insane look in her eyes wasn't telling enough, the bipolar behavior was the nail in the coffin.

"You think I am the one that's crazy?" Barbra's mouth twisted into a smile. "Do you really think someone like my Benjamin, who is so far above your class, would ever truly want to be with someone like *you?*" She laughed a little higher pitched than before. "You're nothing but an experiment, my dear *Holly.*"

The holier than thou demeanor coming from Barbra made Holly's eye start to twitch.

"I guess every man should slum it with a cow before he marries someone closer to his status. You understand, right? Get it out of his system."

Holly bit her bottom lip. Sure, she didn't believe the words out of Barbra's mouth, but that didn't stop the pang of not being good enough that coursed through her body. Holly whole-heartily believed in Ben. He made his feelings toward her clear, but when she'd spent her whole life being looked down upon or being the clumsy one that is there for comic relief, those negative feelings had become ingrained in her. Even if she knew they weren't true, words like that still hit her where they can hurt the most.

"See, you already know the truth." Barbra popped her hip with glee. "You don't think someone like my Benjamin would really be with anyone who looked or acted like you. That's right, he'd never muddy our family tree by adding *you* and your degenerate DNA into it." Her eyes brightened. "I must say, though, I am quite surprised, you're lucky he even remotely pitied you."

The smug look on her face made Holly's blood boil. Sure, there were times she couldn't help but wonder why an Adonis like Ben wanted her, but in the end especially after last night, she knew he was her one. Somewhere along the pages written for them it was spelled out they were meant to be together. Who was Holly to question what the Universe decided?

Holly's fists clenched.

She wasn't, and she was damn sure going to make sure Barbra took her judgmental, bitch of a self and hightailed it out of there.

Clearing her throat, Holly looked Barbra firmly in the eyes. With the tightest smile she could muster, she began, "Funny you should mention that, Barbra. Did you know your son asked me to move in with him this morning?"

"Suck on them apples!" Mildred yelled.

Holding up her hands to stop Barbra from speaking Holly continued, "Not only did I say yes..." Holly took a step closer to the seething woman. "Ben has already *muddied your family line.* Do you want to know how? By consummating our new living arrangements by *nutting* inside me so many goddamn times and might I add without protection. If he didn't knock my *cow* self up there is something seriously wrong."

Barbra's mouth fell opened with disgust, before snapping shut. Her eyes honed in on Holly. "If he did, then you're both fools. No one will ever take him seriously as a Richman if he's ever lumped together with *you*. I hope for your sake and his, you're not as your degenerate self likes to put it, knocked up."

Holly hardened her stance about to tell Barbra Richman off once and for all when an angry voice cut her off.

"I thought I told you to stay away from Holly!" Ben's baritone voice bellowed through the library's entrance.

Holly's eyes snapped to Ben, after hearing his voice. The anger radiated from him. His jaw was firm as his eyes burrowed into his mother's face. If he had been a cartoon, she would've sworn there would have been smoke coming out of his ears.

Huh. That could be funny. Stop it, Holly, this is serious.

She swallowed hard before she focused on Ben's eyes. The hatred she saw there made her stomach bottom out. She'd never seen him this angry, hell she'd never see anyone this angry before.

"Benjamin, what a pleasant surprise," Barbra cooed. Holly didn't miss the slight back step Barbra took away from Ben, though.

Ben held up a paper bag before turning to Holly. "I realized Holly didn't bring lunch today and I wouldn't be able to get away from the clinic later. I needed to make sure she had something to eat." His words were harsh, but the gesture of caring for her well-being melted Holly's heart. How had she end up so lucky to have a man like Ben?

"Question is," Ben continued. "Why are *you* here? I

didn't think you'd actually be stupid enough to not believe me. I thought you were smart. I guess the ivy league diploma is all for show then, huh?" He took a step toward his mother, his body now towered over her.

If Holly didn't already know Ben wouldn't physically hurt another human being she'd be scared for Barbra's life. "She was just leaving," Holly announced, trying to defuse the situation.

"No, she wasn't!" Mildred made her way toward Ben. "This crazy buffoon showed her face here whining about how everything falling apart is Holly's fault and how you were only with her out of pity."

Holly's eyes shot daggers toward Mildred. Didn't the old coot understand it was best to defuse these types of situations rather than add lighter fluid on it? Mentally hitting herself on the head, Holly rolled her eyes.

Of course not.

This was Mildred after all. The old bat lived on drama like this.

Ben's eyes snapped to Holly. When he saw the acknowledgment that she didn't believe Barbra's bullshit, he physically relaxed. He'd never been more thankful in his life than he was at this moment. If he hadn't decided to bring Holly lunch, he would have never walked in on this situation. And, by the stance Holly made he walked in at just the right moment.

Plus, he knew Holly didn't like confrontation and how she'd rather handle everything on her own. Case in point, how she tried to break up with him rather than telling him his bitch of a mother threatened her.

He knew beyond a shadow of a doubt if he'd never shown up at the library, he wouldn't have heard about his mother making an appearance.

Ben's eyes narrowed on Holly.

As soon as this situation was dealt with, he was having a talk with her.

He knew Holly could handle her own, but being in a serious relationship meant not having to handle everything alone. And, he damn well was going to remind her of that.

Images of Holly bent over her desk with her ass in the air, as he made her promise to always talk to him rushed into his mind. Her ass would color nicely.

Not the time.

Pushing the thoughts into the back of his head, he turned his focus on to his mother. Right now, he had bigger things to deal with.

Ben finally understood exactly what he needed to do. It no longer mattered they shared the same bloodline.

Moving to stand in Barbra's personal space Ben's eyes hardened. "I never thought you would be this stupid. I guess, I was wrong. Coming after someone who had nothing to do with your mistakes is fucking ridiculous. Threatening her job, her father, and even her man." He pointed at himself, before shaking his head. "Deep down I always knew you were fucking trash."

"Do not speak to me that way, Benjamin. I'm your mother."

"No. Like I told you yesterday, you aren't." He held out the bag of food. "Take this, Holly."

Holly grabbed it only to throw it in Mildred's outreached arms.

"Free lunch? Don't mind if I do." Mildred snatched the bag from the air.

Ben reached for his phone in his back pocket. "You screwed up, *Barbra*." Using all his control, he took a step away from her. He knew at this point it was best to call Douglas and let him take care of the next steps.

"You fucking bitch!" Holly's words made Ben to snap around only to see his stubborn girlfriend jump for Barbra as his mother lunged for him. "Don't you touch him!" Holly screamed.

"Fuck!" Ben dropped his phone as he ran to where Holly had his mother pinned to the ground.

"I'll have you arrested!" Barbra bellowed at the top of her lungs.

"Not if I kill you. Mildred, help me!"

"I've been waiting for this!" Mildred gleefully rejoiced.

"No." Ben grabbed Holly by the waist pulling her off his mother. Which only resulted in Holly flailing around in his arms, kicking and punching the air. "Let me go, Ben!"

"*No.*" He did his best to hide his laugh as Holly's narrowed eyes directed at him after he placed her on the floor. When Holly's eyes snapped behind his shoulder, he turned his head to see his mother staring at them.

"Yes," Holly demanded. "If this piece of shit is already going to press charges, at least let me get one good hit in." Holly's eyes swam with something he'd never seen before.

Holy shit. In his whole life, no one, other than John had ever shown they'd cared enough to protect him the way Holly was doing right now.

Realization dawned on him.

Holly would risk going to jail in order to protect him. Her father, Waffles, her job, were all thrown out the window the moment he could have potentially been in danger.

Damn, that was hot.

But, also stupid as hell.

Even if she'd tried to jump on him, his mother never stood a chance. What's the most she could have done, pull him to the ground? And then what? He'd wrestled Great Danes that weighed more than his mother on more than one occasion.

"Let me go, now!" She pushed at his chest.

Damn she wanted nothing more than to protect what was hers. He fought his chuckle. "I'm not letting you hit her."

Holly started bouncing around him like a cage fighter without taking her eyes off of her target.

God, he was lucky.

"Why not?" Holly held up her fists.

"Yeah, why not?" Mildred chimed in.

How had these two not gotten into more trouble? He saw Mildred from the corner of his eye trying to egg Holly on.

"I'm pressing charges." Barbra stood, before fixing her skirt.

"No, you're not," Ben growled.

"Why, yes I am." With her words, Barbra smoothed her hair before pulling out her phone.

"I will kill you where you stand!" Holly's voice echoed through the lobby as she swung her fist in the air. She must have had a little too much oomph behind it since Holly ended up spinning in a circle.

"I'll hold her down!" Mildred happily offered to help.

For Christ's sake!

In fear of letting Holly free, he decided he needed to end this once and for all. Quickly turning to face his mother, while he kept Holly securely behind him, Ben spoke, "I'll only say this once, Barbra. You have twenty-four hours to leave. Leave this town and everything you know behind. I'll see to Richmond Industries being handed over to the board. You've got one chance to make it out of here without ending up in a jumpsuit. One phone call and everything gets sent to the proper people."

Barbra's eyes hardened.

"And to make myself clear one final time, I can and *will* destroy you."

For the first time since battling his mother, Ben saw the resignation in her eyes. This time she knew he wouldn't hesitate in putting an end to her.

"Fine." She moved closer to him. "You want me gone, you've got it. I'm gone. Listen to me, little boy, the moment you allow someone like *her* into your life, *you* lose everything."

"The only person losing everything here is you."

Barbra sneered.

"You have twenty-four hours."

With a huff, Barbra turned on her heel ready to exit. When she made it to the door, she turned to Holly. "I hope you're happy knowing you're destroying a family."

Ben moved into Barbra's line of sight. "No, Barbra, she's *made* a family."

His mother's lips curled as she growled. She looked him up and down once more before hastily leaving the building.

Once the door shut behind her, Ben finally let his body relax.

"Well damn, who needs coffee when you get a show like that?" Mildred plopped another chip in her mouth.

Seeing Holly's lunch almost gone, Ben made a mental note to have a pizza delivered at noon for Holly. These two are going to be the death of him. Moving to his discarded phone, he picked it up before he started thumbing through it.

"Umm, uhh, thank you for the lunch, or what's left of it." Holly bit her bottom lip. The uncertainty in her eyes broke him.

"Come here, Grace." Instead of her normal protest at the name she willingly walked into his arms. Ben kissed the top of her head as he rubbed her back. "I love you, baby."

"Didn't I say you make my life a freakin' roller coaster?" Holly asked, resting her head on his chest.

"I think you might've mentioned it."

"In case you didn't realize what I was referring to..." She gestured to the doors which made Ben laugh.

"I know, baby, but guess what?" He kissed the top of her head. "Sometimes a roller coaster can be fun, and the best part, from now on, we'll get to ride these roller coasters together."

"Until your crazy mother shows up again." Ben saw the hint of panic in her eyes. "I don't want to keep dealing with her. What if she tries going after my dad?"

"Won't happen."

"What makes you so sure about that?"

Ben held his phone to Holly. "I might have lied on the twenty-four hour part. I may or may not have contacted the private investigator this morning to get the ball rolling."

"My kind of man!" Mildred threw one of her fists in the air as she took a bite of Holly's sandwich with the other.

"Mine too." Holly stood on her tiptoes bringing her lips to his.

CHAPTER TWENTY-ONE

TWO MONTHS LATER

BEN SAT BACK on his knees on the newly finished porch watching as Holly played with the dogs in the backyard. When he heard the screen door shut, he knew Henry had made his way out to them. Over the past couple of weeks, it'd become a routine.

Ben would work around the house repairing what needed to be fixed while Henry guided him through every step. Holly would take care of the chores before feeding the dogs and packing meals for the week. She'd order them dinner, or Ben would help Henry cook on the grill.

After they ate, Holly would always insist on going out to the backyard to play with Ripley and Waffles, while Ben finished whatever project he had at hand. Somewhere along the evening, Henry would come out to the porch and sit next to Ben. Sometimes, they sat in silence, other times Henry told stories of his past.

The stories were always Ben's favorite. He'd quietly work as Henry retold stories of his wife, his years working, and of Holly.

The ones about Holly Ben liked the most. He couldn't

help but picture a round faced Holly as she ran throughout the backyard causing havoc as she tripped and stumbled on invisible objects.

From his spot on the porch Ben glanced at the woman that had captured his heart. Currently, she sat on the ground while Lord Waffles ran around her in circles while Ripley sat directly in front of her waiting patiently for Holly to throw the tennis ball.

A chuckle escaped his lips as he shook his head at their antics.

This was perfection.

"One day, I come out here and you'll be in the yard with Holly playing with your children," Henry stated.

Henry smiled wide as he watched Holly playing with the dogs.

"One day," Ben agreed. That was another thing he'd grown accustomed to. Henry's not so subtle hints that he wanted to see both of them married and with children. He couldn't blame him, as the days went on, Ben wanted the same things.

Every night when he came home from the clinic to Holly in their kitchen trying not to burn the place down, or if she was curled up on the couch with Twitch at her side, made him feel whole.

Not the her burning their dinner, but her being there. In their *home*.

Ben laughed to himself thinking back to the nights he'd come home to find Holly in the kitchen. He found out early on she was *not* a cook.

Hell, Holly couldn't cook even if her life depended on it. Oh man, when they were moving her into his house, as a gesture to everyone that helped, Holly decided to sneak away and make everyone lunch. John and Ben, along with

Henry's supervision, had worked the whole day getting her stuff in so she wanted to do something nice for them.

Three hours later a used fire extinguisher, and burnt chicken tenders was the outcome Ben realized how dangerous Holly was in the kitchen. So he made a deal with her. Ben would handle anything that involved any sort of cooking appliance or fire and she could do everything else.

He *thought* it was a foolproof compromise. How could she hurt herself or the house making a sandwich or cutting vegetables, right?

One emergency trip to his clinic later where he stitched up her sliced finger, told him otherwise.

Laughing at the memory, he shrugged his shoulders. Not everyone needed to know how to cook, and he could say for sure, whenever she tried, he found himself on some whirlwind ride. But, he wouldn't change any of it.

"There she goes again," Henry spoke, as Holly threw the tennis ball in the air. When Holly ran after it along with the dogs, she tripped. Thankfully, she caught herself, though. "She's definitely gotten good over the years at catching herself."

"I've witnessed it," Ben agreed. "Remember when she brought the box of dishes from her apartment to the house? She tripped up the steps. Instead of falling and breaking everything in the box, she did some weird ninja move where she spun around. She then ended up with her back on the side of the railing her and the box unharmed." Ben laughed at the memory. He still didn't know how she managed it, but she did.

A red hue appeared on his cheeks as he images of last night poured into his mind. After coming, as Holly tried to dismount from his dick, her whole body shifted weird and she toppled off the bed. On the way down, though, she somehow grabbed every sheet to cushion her fall.

He panicked at first that she'd hurt herself, but when he looked over the side of the bed, she laid there tangled in blankets, her hair a mess, and her face red.

Nope. She wasn't hurt. Instead, she had the biggest smile on her face that he'd ever seen. She took pride in knowing she was fast on her feet. When it came to her as she liked to put it, her 'clumsy award.'

Yep, living with Holly had shown Ben just how resourceful *and* clumsy she truly was.

Waffles bark snapped him out of his thoughts. He sat back on his heels as he watched Holly throw the ball.

Life was perfect.

"Ben, I want to talk to you about something," Henry remarked.

"Shoot."

"I know you paid off the mortgage on the house along with taking care of my medical bills. But, I wanted to make a deal of some sort." Henry sat on the rocking chair as Ben worked on replacing a rotted piece of wood on the railing.

"How many times are we going to have this conversation? You don't need to pay me back."

"I know you keep saying that, but it doesn't sit well with me that you paid all that money out of your own pocket."

Ben wanted to roll his eyes. It was almost the same exact conversation each time they'd end up alone. "I'm not taking any money from you."

"Why not?"

Ben resigned himself before turning entirely to Henry. "You don't take money from family. That's why. When I lost my dad, I never thought I'd have a father figure or any type of

parent in my life again. We all know how shitty Barbra was."
He shook his head. "When my dad died, I thought I was
pretty much an orphan in a weird sort of way. I had no one to
go to. My dad was the one who supported me. He did everything in his power to help me achieve my goals of owning my
own veterinary practice. He was the one I turned to when I
had trouble or when I needed advice. He was always there
for me... until he wasn't. I know you aren't my actual father,
and I'm freakin' grateful for that or me sleeping with Holly
would open up a whole new can of worms. But, in a weird
way, you've stepped into that father role that I was missing."

Henry's eyes widened. "Ben, I didn't know."

"How could you? I've never said anything. Here's the
thing, Henry, you're a good man. One of the best I have ever
known. You've got integrity and a good heart. You care for
everyone."

"Not your bitch of a mother."

Ben huffed out a laugh. "Point taken. Regardless, you're
my family. You, Holly, all the animals, and whoever else
comes along. From here on out we have each other's backs.
Family takes care of family."

Henry's eyes lit. "When you came into Holly's life I
knew you were the one for her. You made her happy and
you took care of her. Since you've shown up she hasn't
stopped smiling. The first day I met you I knew you'd be
good for her. That's also the day I first saw you as a son,
Ben."

Well, shit.

Ben didn't know what to say. Feelings and emotions
were never his strong suit. But then again, words weren't
needed.

Ben turned back to his task of fixing the railing as they

settled into silence. It felt good to have a "dad" again. Especially, one that reminded him so much of his own.

Another five minutes passed until, Henry finally spoke, "I might not be okay with the fact you paid so much money, but I'll stop bringing it up."

"You can keep bringing it up if you want, but you'll always get the same answer." Ben laughed.

Scratching his fingers along his chin, Henry squinted his eyes. "Maybe I can make it up with an exchange. Whenever you and Holly want some free time, I want the pups."

A ridiculously broad smile appeared on Ben's face. "Sounds like a deal to me."

"Good." Henry sat back in his chair and watched as Holly played with the dogs.

Hopefully, now they'd come to an agreement.

Ben went back to work as Henry stared into the backyard watching Holly.

A few minutes went by before Henry cleared his throat getting Ben's attention. "I'm not going to be around forever, son," he spoke softly. "Lord knows after everything I've been through I shouldn't be here now... but, I know there is a reason why I am."

Ben focused his full attention on Henry as he cocked his head to the side. "And what do you think that reason is?"

Henry watched Holly as she moved through the backyard before he turned to Ben. That's when Ben saw his eyes glossy with unshed tears. "To walk my little girl down the aisle to you."

Holly tossed the ball again for Ripley and Waffles. She couldn't help but laugh when Waffles fell over himself running after the ball.

Like mother, like son.

After making sure Waffles didn't hurt himself, she looked behind her. Ben and her father sat on the porch and talked much like they did every time they came over.

The first couple of evenings she'd sat with them as Ben worked on whatever project he was commissioned on for the time being. However, her idea of a good time did not include her father nitpicking everything Ben touched. Nor did it involve the dogs getting underfoot and constantly worrying about them. Instead she made it a point to take the dogs into the yard and give them all some much needed exercise.

Holly watched as her father pointed to something Ben was fixing. Ben liked the guidance from Henry. He never once complained. Instead, he soaked up the knowledge and was grateful for it.

The pride Holly saw on Ben's face once a project was completed made her heart skip. He'd always wait for her father's approval of his work. Once he got the, "job well done, son," he'd beam. Seeing Ben's expression matched a child getting approval from a father. It only made her love him more.

When a wet nose hit her leg, she looked down to see Ripley drop the ball at her feet. "You want me to throw it again, Pretty Girl?"

Ripley barked while jumping around in circles, which made Waffles do the same. "Will you let your brother actually get the ball this time?"

"You know she won't."

Holly turned to see her father making his way over to them.

"What are you doing out here?" she asked, before

tossing the ball.

"I wanted to come see you. I told Ben to finish up the handrail."

Holly looked at him sideways. "And you didn't want to be there to guide him?"

Henry screeched his chin. "I may have also left him with his thoughts."

"And what thoughts are those?"

"None of your concern, Pumpkin. Now, why don't you drop the third degree and tell me how you are?" He gave her his lopsided smile.

This time she really did look skeptical of her father. "What's going on, Dad? You already know how I am."

"I know, Pumpkin. I just wanted to check on you. You've been living with that big oaf a while now. I wanted to make sure everything was to your standards. Do I need to threaten Ben with my "I know people in the mafia" speech?"

Holly lightly pushed her father's shoulder. "No, you don't." She laughed shaking her head no.

"I could. You don't know who I know."

Holly cocked her brow. "Seriously Dad, what's this all about?"

Henry smiled. "I'm happy for you, Pumpkin."

"I'm happy too, Dad." Her smile matched his.

Holly picked up the ball Ripley had placed at her feet and threw it before jogging with the dogs to get it.

"Good. Now, when can I get some grandbabies?"

Holly instantly tripped over an invisible rock before finding herself face first on the ground. She rolled onto her back before she pushed herself into the sitting position. That's when she saw Ben sprinting toward her while her father doubled over in laughter.

CHAPTER TWENTY-TWO

HOLLY PARKED her car in the driveway of her and Ben's home. Even though it had been over two months, she still couldn't believe she lived with him. In a house, nonetheless.

Once his mother was out of the picture, everything fell into place. The move was easy, minus a situation with burnt chicken tenders that was blown way out of proportion, if you asked her.

All of her belongings felt right amongst Ben's. It was like they were always meant to be. Also Holly started writing again. She didn't quite know if she felt confident enough to actually publish a story, but she was having a good time writing.

Walking toward the path to the front door, she noticed what looked like brown dog treats laying on the ground. Bending over she picked one up.

"Why's this here?"

Looking ahead, she noticed more dog treats in a line leading up the front steps. "What the hell?"

Instead of picking them up, she decided to follow the path curious as to what was going on. When she reached the front door, she opened it. The treats continued on a path into the living room. Throwing her belongings on the table by the door, she moved through the room to follow them.

Holly froze when she reached the living room.

In front of her on the floor was a massive heart made out of dog treats. In the middle, stood Ben. At his side, Ripley waited patiently, while Waffles on the other hand, was munching on the right side of the heart. Slowly making his way around to all the treats.

"Waffles," Ben growled. "Get back into formation. We've practiced this for days!"

Waffles reluctantly looked at Ben and then the treats. After one last longing look toward his goodies, he slowly padded next to Ben and plopped onto his butt with a huff.

"Why are you such a piece of work?" Ben asked before scratching the little guy between the ears.

Twitch not wanting to be left out, made his way to stand between Ben's legs, his head twitching every few seconds.

Holly's hand flew to her mouth at the sight in front of her.

Her family.

From the corner of her eye, she saw lit candles and roses scattered throughout the entire room. She looked at Ben, who presented her with a lopsided grin.

"Hey, baby." Ben winked.

"Ben?"

As Holly took a step forward, he held out his hands. "Stay right there."

"What's going on?"

Ben cocked his head to the side as a chuckle escaped his lips. "Now, Grace, you and I both know what's going on."

Holly's mouth fell open as her eyes widened.

Ignoring her reaction, Ben lowered himself to his knee.

Is this really happening?

Ben pulled out a tiny box from his pocket.

Yep, this was happening.

When Ben opened it, she saw the ring.

"Oh shit."

"Only you, Grace." He laughed before he cleared his throat. "Holly Flanagan, you came into my life like a tornado. One moment you were standing, the next you were on the ground with blood all over your face."

"Your fault," she was quick to interject.

"Yes, technically it was my fault but don't forget I *did* yell watch out." He smirked. "Who knew your klutziness and quick wit would turn me on?"

"Really? Can you not be serious even at a time like this?" She placed her hands on her hips.

"I am being serious. When I had you on the exam table looking at your tooth, I almost lost my shit. I wanted you then just as bad as I want you now."

"Ben," she warned.

"Fine. I won't mention how you get me harder than I've ever been in my life." Her glare made him laugh. "But, it's your love for animals that really sealed the deal. When you found out about Twitch, you were more concerned about the kitten than my ditching you."

"You didn't ditch me, you were saving lives."

"And that right there is another reason I fell in love with you. Grace, you complete me. After my dad died, I never was whole again. I walked around aimlessly just going through the motions, but when you brought hurricane Holly into the picture, I finally felt whole again. I felt right. *You* make me feel right." He gestured around him. "We now live together in this home with our four-legged children. Holly, I hate to break this to you but I think it's about time we made it official. Waffles keeps telling all the other dogs his mommy and daddy only live together but aren't married."

Holly raised her brow. "And what's wrong with that? People can live together and not be married. There is absolutely nothing wrong with that."

"I agree there isn't a thing wrong with it." Ben laughed. "But, Waffles also let it slip he wanted to see his mommy in a beautiful white dress and him in a tuxedo. In reality though, I think he's only pushing for us to get hitched so that he can strut his stuff in a tux."

Holly looked at Waffles who'd sneakily made his way back to the edge of the heart where he started eating the dog treats again. "I wouldn't put that past him."

"And Ripley wants to put on a doggie dress to match her momma."

She nodded. "And what do you want?"

"I want to spend the rest of my life with you. I want to fill this house with animals and kids. I want you to be my wife, the mother of my children, and my partner for the rest of our lives."

Holly crossed her arms over her chest, with a smile. "And what do I get out of it?"

"Me."

Holly ran into his open arms making him fall onto his back. "Watch out for Twitch!" He pulled their cat from behind him and placed Twitch out of harm's way.

The look of annoyance on Twitch's face had Holly biting back a laugh. Thankfully, Twitch had seen the danger coming toward him and moved out of the way on his own. That didn't stop his judgmental glare shot their way though.

Once Holly saw Twitch make his way out of the room, she turned back to the only man that would ever own her heart. "I love you, Ben."

"Is that a yes?" he asked, his eyes hopeful as he stared at her.

"You haven't asked me anything yet," she joked, while kissing the side of his cheek.

"So picky. Fine. Holly Flanagan, will you marry me? Will you put me and Waffles out of our misery and do me the honor of becoming my wife?"

Holly tapped her index finger on her chin. "I'll think about it."

Ben growled, before he rolled her onto her back as she laughed. "I'll give you something to think about." He started tickling her showing zero mercy. When Holly started flailing around on the ground, the dogs started to bark and play, running around them in circles.

"Yes, Ben, yes!" She held her sides, trying to get him to stop tickling her. "I'll marry you!"

"I never had any doubt." He finally stopped his ambush before he leaned in and kissed her.

After a few seconds, Holly pulled away from Ben's lips. She glanced at what remained of the dog treats on the floor. Waffles was on his belly crawling from treat to treat as he went around the heart eating. "Why the dog treats?" she asked, with a laugh as she saw Ripley doing the same on the other side.

"I thought it was a perfect choice. We did after all, meet in the dog park." He kissed her neck.

"Where you hit me in the face with a Frisbee." Ben glared at her. "What? Don't glare at me. You did!"

Ben placed his hand behind her neck before bringing his lips to hers. "And I wouldn't have it any other way."

"Damn straight."

They laid on the floor laughing while the dogs cleaned up the treats. Holly looked around the room and smiled. This was exactly where she wanted to be.

Holly moved herself onto her elbows, when she saw something that grabbed her attention. "Ben, why is there a baby gate around the cat tree?"

Ben glared at Waffles, before answering, "Talk to your son."

"What do you mean talk to my son?"

"I got tired of coming in here after hearing him whine." Holly cocked her brow.

"He'd somehow managed to get himself stuck on the top of the cat tree. He thinks if he can reach the cat treats, that means they are his for the taking. I only placed them that high for Twitch *thinking* they'd be safe." Ben shook his head. "He climbed up there and ate them fine, but Lord Waffles has no idea how to get back down."

Holly burst out laughing before she called Waffles into her lap. "That so, little guy? Is your daddy tired of you stealing all the cat treats?"

"No," Ben answered. "I'm tired of having to put his ass back on the floor."

"It's not his fault he has short legs." Holly scratched Waffles' belly.

"He gets up onto the tree fine, doesn't he?"

"We all have our talents."

"And his revolves around food."

Holly placed her hands over Waffles ears to shield him. "Hey, be nice!"

"I am being nice. I didn't say I didn't love him."

Holly's mouth broke into a smile as she laughed. "What a crazy family we are."

"And we wouldn't have it any other way." Ben plucked Holly from her spot on the floor and placed her into his lap. "Now, let's celebrate." He didn't give her a chance to say anything before he kissed her lips.

CHAPTER TWENTY-THREE

ONE MONTH LATER

HOLLY PACED AROUND the living room of her father's house trying her best to remain calm. As she let her mind wander, she realized how much work Ben had accomplished. The house looked just as it did when she was younger. If not better.

Ben with her father's watchful eye, really did a great job of restoring the bungalow.

Pay attention!

She had bigger things to focus her attention on.

In less than ten minutes, she was supposed to walk out of the back door and down the porch steps into Ben's arms.... to become his wife.

His wife.

Holy shit, Holly Flanagan was about to become someone's wife.

Ben's wife to be more exact.

Holly never thought she'd be here. But, here she was, about to marry the man of her dreams.

"You okay, Pumpkin?" Henry asked, as he walked into the living room.

Whoa.

Holly was momentarily taken aback by her father's appearance. She'd forgotten how handsome he cleaned up. Henry stood before her with bright eyes and a lopsided grin in a perfectly tailored tux.

Holly looked down at her dress. If her father looked this good, Ben would look ten times better. She'd never be able to compare. Biting her bottom lip, she looked at her dad. "Do I look okay?"

"More breathtaking than your mother on our wedding day," he answered, tears in his eyes. "But, Pumpkin, if the hole on the floor from your pacing is any indication of your state of being, I would say something is wrong." He moved to sit on the couch, before focusing his attention on her. "What's got you all up in arms?"

Before she knew it, Holly started pacing again. "This is really happening, Dad."

"It is."

"I'm about to marry the love of my life."

"That is a good thing, Pumpkin. If you are going to marry someone, you want them to be the love of your life."

At his words, she stopped pacing and glared at him. How could he not comprehend her dilemma here? Didn't he understand what was going on? Holly crossed her arms over her chest. "What if I make a fool of myself?"

When Henry bite back his smile, her eye started to twitch.

With a small shake of his head Henry stood. "How so?"

Absentmindedly Holly started pacing again. "I don't know. What if I'm at some veterinarian function with Ben and I do something stupid like spill red sauce down the front of my dress? Or, what if I try to make chicken tenders again and I burn down our house?"

"That's a simple fix. Don't make chicken tenders anymore. "

"Dad..." she warned.

Before she could say anything else, he continued, "And as for you spilling something on your dress, do you really think Ben would care about something like that?"

"No." She shook her head. "He wouldn't. If he knew it bothered me, he would probably spill something on his shirt to match."

"Exactly." Henry clapped his hands together. "So, then what's the problem?"

Holly bit her bottom lip.

"Tell me, Holly. What's got you freaking out?"

She lifted the bottom of her wedding dress. "What if I fall? I have no idea why I thought it would be a good idea for me to get married in heels and in the backyard at that. I'm gonna break my neck before I ever say I do!"

Henry threw his head back as he barked out a deep laugh. "Well, damn."

Holly glared at him. He might be her father, but no one laughs at a bride on their wedding day. She calculated how fast she could get Mildred to speak to one of her contacts.

"Put those daggers away, little girl. I'm only laughing because I now owe Ben ten bucks."

Holly's eye started to twitch. "What do you mean you owe him ten dollars?"

Henry walked over to a spare bag on the floor. "Ben bet me ten dollars you'd freak out about your choice of footwear. Something about your stubborn ways and demanding you wear heels like every other bride." Henry pulled out a pair of Holly's favorite work flats. "He packed these for you."

A part of Holly wanted to yell at him for not believing

she could walk in the heels, but a bigger part of her sighed in relief.

See, this just proved how perfect Ben truly was for her. Not only did he know she would freak out but he brought her an option to change into. She was one hundred percent marrying the right man. However, she still planned on giving him shit for it regardless. A small smile appeared on her face. She knew a way he could make it up to her.

"Put these on, and let's get this party started," her father remarked while handing the shoes to her. "I'm gonna make sure Waffles is in place."

After Henry left the room, Holly sat on the couch smiling as she slipped on her favorite pair of work flats. Righting herself once she was done, she fixed her dress before making her way to the back door.

This was it.

Today she married the love of her life.

The moment Holly stepped outside, Henry held out his good arm so she could hook her arm with his.

"Better?" he asked, before kissing her on the cheek.

"Much." Holly took a deep breath as she turned away from him and started down their makeshift aisle.

That's when she finally saw Ben. Instantly everything felt right in world.

Ben stood under the archway he'd built only a few weekends ago. He took her breath away. He looked every bit of the Adonis as she thought he was the first day they'd met. Pure happiness rush through her body as Ripley sat by his side in a pink dress. John stood behind Ripley, as Ben's *human* best man.

Holly smiled when she saw Ripley had a thin leash in her mouth that attached to one sleeping Twitch at her feet.

Oh, did he? Holly looked back to Ben who winked her way.

Leave it to him to somehow include the whole family.

Perfect.

It was a small wedding. Only a few people were in attendance. In the chairs on either side of the pathway sat some of the board members for Richman Industries that Ben had become good friends with as he helped with the transition. On the opposite side sat Mildred and her husband.

Holly had to laugh at Mildred's outfit. She wore one of the biggest hats she'd ever seen. Her poor husband kept getting hit in the head with the thing.

Typical Mildred.

Then sitting only a few feet in front of Holly in the middle of the aisle was Lord Waffles. He looked so hand-some in his doggie tux as his tongue flopped out of the side of his mouth. She had to fight the urge to run for her phone to take a picture of him. Her heart skipped when she realized he even had on a black bow tie.

"You ready to marry that man waitin' over there?" Henry's voice brought her back to reality.

Holly's eyes once again went straight to Ben. His grin spoke volumes as he watched her from afar. The love that poured from him made her feel like everything was going to be okay. Always. She had to stop herself from running into his arms.

Holly couldn't wait another second to be by his side. "Let's do this."

Henry squeezed her hand before he signaled for Waffles to start walking. Once he was a few steps ahead of them, they followed suit.

Through the entire time the music played, Holly couldn't take her eyes off Ben.

Who said real life wasn't like romance novels? Her life was a romance novel come to life.

Score one for the big girls!

They stopped a few feet from Ben where her father leaned over and kissed her cheek. "Go get your man, Pumpkin."

Holly smiled brightly. "I plan to." Stepping out of her father's embrace, she started moving toward Ben, her full focus on him.

Unfortunately for her, though, she didn't noticed Waffles had stopped walking. Before she knew it, Holly found herself stumbling through the air. She placed her hands out in front of her, trying her best to cushion her impact.

Closing her eyes, she cursed her clumsiness, ready for the hit.

The impact never came though.

Instead, Holly found herself in Ben's arms before she hit the ground. When she opened her eyes, she was neatly tucked in Ben's embrace.

Ben shook his head as he chuckled before he kissed her. "What am I going to do with you, Grace?" His face glowed with happiness as he smoothed some of her hair behind her ear.

Holly gave him a half smile, as she watched his eyes filled with love that she was sure matched her own. "Always catch me."

Did you enjoy Ben and Holly's story? If so, their story continues in Stumbling Into Forever. Read on for a sneak peek of chapter one!

STUMBLING INTO FOREVER
CHAPTER ONE

"Drop that donut right now, Waffles, or so help me I'm gonna murder you *and* enjoy it!"

Ben Richman heard his wife, Holly, yelling from their kitchen. With a chuckle and a shake of his head, he removed their cat Twitch from his lap and made his way through the house to investigate.

What has she gotten herself into now? A smirk spread across his face.

"Don't you run away from me, Waffles! That's mine and you know it!" The growl Ben heard coming from Holly had him laughing. Leave it to her to argue with a dog. Then again, this was Lord Waffles they were talking about. Arguing with him was a must, as Ben had come to find out since meeting Holly and her overly opinionated, high and mighty Corgi.

As Ben rounded the corner, he saw his oh so graceful wife running around the kitchen island chasing after their dog.

The same dog that just so happened to have Holly's last donut in his mouth.

As Waffles ran past the spot where Ben stood, the dog had the gall to eye him, almost begging to get the crazy lady to stop chasing him.

Figures.

Ben rolled his eyes. He'd be lying if he didn't say there was a part of him that wanted to watch the catastrophe he was sure was about to happen. Everyone knew whatever Waffles wanted, Waffles got, and if that meant destroying everything in his wake, or taking his mother's last donut, even though he knew he'd be staring death in the eyes, he'd do it. Everyone was beneath Waffles, and that dog made sure they knew it. Including his mother, who clearly wanted that last donut bad enough, she'd fight for it.

Ben shook his head with a sigh. As much as he'd like to watch the explosion there was another part of him, a bigger part, that wanted to make sure no one ended up on the floor in a pile of blood because they banged their head against the countertop.

And by no one, he meant Holly.

Better get this over with. "Grace, stop chasing him before you end up on your ass." Ben laughed as he stepped into the kitchen.

Ben had learned a thing or two after being married to Holly for the better part of a year and there was no doubt in his mind what was coming next.

Prepared, Ben strategically placed his hands out in front of him.

Within seconds, Holly came barreling into his arms at full speed. Although Ben was ready, he somehow lost his footing causing them both to cascade onto the floor with a loud oomph.

"Ahh!" Holly screamed as they landed.

The moment they were on the floor she tried to jump

off him. You know that fight-or-flight instinct? Ben wasn't having any of it though. He held onto her hips keeping her locked in place on top of him.

"What on earth am I going to do with you, Grace?" Ben chuckled, as he helped Holly straighten herself so she was now straddling his waist.

"Where in the world did you freakin' come from?" Holly huffed while she pushed her auburn hair out of her face. She didn't wait for an answer as she scanned the room for any sign of his holiness.

As if on cue, Lord Waffles walked past them with the donut in his mouth and an extra pep in his step.

Holly growled as she narrowed her eyes at the betraying bastard. The moment Waffles shot her a wink, Ben had to stop her from lunging.

Ben's brows shot to the ceiling when Waffles winked at him too.

Waffles freaking *winked* at him.

No matter how many times he'd seen Waffles demand his peasants listen to him, Ben still couldn't believe it. For a dog, he sure did have a lot of quirks. In the name of veterinary medicine, maybe he should study him, possibly resea–

"You knew that was mine!" Holly made a second lunge for Waffles as he happily chomped on his treasure taunting her.

Thank God Ben's reflexes were sharp, that's what happens after spending years wrestling Rottweilers. And clearly, Holly couldn't be trusted not to strangle their dog right now.

In one swift movement, Ben grabbed onto Holly's hips flipping her onto her back and under him with ease. "It's too late now, Grace. You wouldn't want it after he's slobbered all over it anyway."

"Says you!" Holly glared at him. "That was my last peanut butter and glazed donut. I've been saving it until I reached my word count. He knew that! We talked about it in great detail when I was struggling to hit my next two thousand words. He did this on purpose." Holly's eyes snapped to Waffles who was swallowing the last bite before licking his lips. "I'm gonna remember this the next time you need something." She glared at him before she threw her head back onto the floor in defeat. "That was my donut."

The pout that spread across Holly's mouth had Ben laughing.

And he wondered where Waffles got his flair for the dramatics?

"I'll buy you more." He laughed kissing Holly lightly on the lips. As Ben looked down at his wife, a smile ran across his face. He still couldn't believe how lucky he was to have found Holly. He still couldn't believe how lucky he was to have found Holly. Even though that meeting involved her getting hit in the face with a rogue Frisbee, which now knowing Holly wasn't all that surprising. She was, after all, a master at tripping on thin air, falling over, and if you looked up the word klutz in the dictionary, you'd see a picture of her, with the title walking disaster under it. But to him, she was absolutely perfect in every way. From her lush hips down to the deep hunter green of her eyes.

Holly was made for him.

"It won't be the same," Holly groaned as she pushed the palm of her hand to his chest and gave a nudge. "And stop calling me Grace! You jumped in front of me. It was *your* fault I ended up crashing into you. Not mine. What was I supposed to do? You came out of freakin' nowhere!"

Ben threw his head back and burst out laughing,

causing Holly to let out a growl. That only made him laugh harder. "I don't know, Grace. How about stop?"

"As if I could stop. Once this load starts a-movin' nothing is stopping it."

"Excuse me?" Ben's brows shot to the ceiling.

Panic flashed through Holly's eyes.

Good. After all this time you should know better than to say shit like that.

Before Ben could say anything more, Ripley came bouncing into the kitchen, with Twitch right on her tail.

"Oh, oh, Ripley, baby girl, come save your momma," Holly cooed at their other dog, Ripley, their Australian shepherd.

Ripley quickly made her way over to Holly's face and started licking. "That's not saving me!" Holly squirmed as she did her best to avoid the onslaught of kisses coming from Ripley.

That's when Ben felt something nudge his arm. He looked down to see Twitch — rightly named so because of the slight twitch he has in his head from some punk kid poisoning him when he was a kitten.

Twitch jumped onto Holly's chest trying to lick her face just as Ripley was, making Ben laugh again.

Somewhere along the lines, Twitch had taken to Ripley like she was his own mother and converted himself into being a dog.

Where Ripley went. Twitch went.

Whatever Ripley did. Twitch did.

Ben's heart warmed at the memories of Ripley and Waffles play fighting and Twitch trying to jump in and hold his own. The play fighting only lasted a few seconds before Ripley would grab Twitch in her mouth and take him away from the fight.

Go figure. Protective. Just like Holly.

Although right now, Holly looked more like she wanted to throttle Waffles rather than protect him.

Twitch looked at Ripley before assessing they were still kissing their mother. So, he dove back in.

At this point, Ben was positive all their animals were certifiably insane. And with their ringmaster, Lord Waffles, with plans of world domination, calling most of the shots he'd given up trying to make any sense of it.

And he wouldn't have it any other way.

Life was always an adventure between their pets and Holly.

Oh, and Ben couldn't forget Mildred. Holly's completely inappropriate older coworker at the local library. Whenever Mildred was around, things *always* got interesting.

Ben pushed himself off Holly before grabbing onto her arms yanking her to her feet. "Up you go, Grace."

"I'm gonna put arsenic in your dinner tonight."

"That'd be a welcomed taste with your cooking." At Holly's narrowed eyes he barked out a laugh. "Come on. You know it's true. Sexy, talented, outspoken, kindhearted, feisty, best writer in the world you are, a chef you ain't. Or do you want me to bring up the time you almost burnt the house down when you tried to make chicken tenders?"

Another growl came from Holly. "That wasn't my fault!"

"Yes, my bad, that's right it was the chicken's fault."

"Damn right it was! Plus, I was only trying to be nice and feed you and John 'cause you guys were working hard moving my crap in."

"Oh, we got a break from moving your shit in when we

had to call the fire department." Ben smirked at her narrowed eyes and thinned lips.

"Am I ever going to live that down?"

"No." Ben's eyes twinkled with amusement. "Hey, at least I'm not as bad as John."

Annoyed Holly jerked herself away from him and grabbed her bag. "You and John can kiss my ass."

When she started for the front door Ben hollered after her, "Where do you think you're going?"

From over her shoulder, Holly shot him an evil look. "Out to get more donuts."

At the word "donut" Waffles ran to Holly's side and started jumping. Well, if you can consider whatever Waffles does with his tiny little legs jumping.

"Not for you!" Holly sidestepped Waffles shooting her glare from Ben to their dog.

Holly almost made it all the way to the front door without an incident.

Almost.

As she moved through the hallway, she tripped over an invisible crack and stumbled. Without looking back at Ben, she quickly righted herself before blowing her hair out of her face.

Ben did a quick assessment of her to make sure she was okay. When he realized she was fine, he let out a laugh.

As Ben opened his mouth to tell her to bring him back some donuts too, Holly did what she was known for. She tripped over the entranceway and nearly fell right out of the door.

Ben had to bite back his joy, as his smile spread from ear to ear. *Never a dull moment.*

Holly straightened herself with a huff as she hiked her

bag higher onto her shoulder. Once she was composed, she turned to face him with narrowed eyes. "Not. A. Word."

Ben held his hands up in surrender as he bit his lip, trying and failing to keep from laughing.

The second Holly turned from him and stomped out of the door, he shouted, "And you wonder why I'll never stop calling you Grace!"

Continue their story in Stumbling Into Forever.

ALSO BY MOLLY O'HARE

Hollywood Hopeful Series

Hollywood Dreams

Risking It All (Danny and Lexi's Story) – *Coming soon*

Stumbling Through Life Series

Stumbling Into Him – *This book*

Stumbling Into Forever

Teased Series

Teased by Fire

Lucas and Miranda's story coming soon

Standalone Books

Nothing But a Dare

Learning Curves

Stay up to date on New Releases

Sign up for my newsletter by clicking the link or going to my website:

MollyOHareauthor.com

Check out the Fun Facts on the next page

ABOUT THE AUTHOR

Much like any author out there, sleeping does not come easily to me. It turns out I have the worst insomnia of anyone I have ever met. Since I was a little girl, to help myself fall asleep, I would recite stories. Each night I would pick up where the story left off previously until the tale was complete. One morning, after I finished a particularly fun story, I decided I wanted to start sharing them with others. A few months later, here I am, sharing my lack of sleep with all of you. Who says the stories in our heads can't be fun for others?

I think I will bestow upon you some fun facts about me.

Fun Facts for Stumbling Into Him:
I have a Corgi
I love pickles
I am a savory rather than sweet person
I got to pet a goat in March. (I am still riding this high!)
I get lost in the rabbit hole which is makeup tutorials, but I have *zero* idea how to do makeup
I tripped up the stairs this morning... Don't worry, this a normal occurrence for me
I want to live in a log cabin somewhere it snows

Stay Connected

Made in the USA
Columbia, SC
31 January 2021

32029437R00131